BEFORE HE PREYS

(A MACKENZIE WHITE MYSTERY—BOOK 9)

BLAKE PIERCE

BOOKS BY BLAKE PIERCE

THE MAKING OF RILEY PAIGE SERIES
WATCHING (Book #1)

RILEY PAIGE MYSTERY SERIES
ONCE GONE (Book #1)
ONCE TAKEN (Book #2)
ONCE CRAVED (Book #3)
ONCE LURED (Book #4)
ONCE HUNTED (Book #5)
ONCE PINED (Book #6)
ONCE FORSAKEN (Book #7)
ONCE COLD (Book #8)
ONCE STALKED (Book #9)
ONCE LOST (Book #10)
ONCE BURIED (Book #11)
ONCE BOUND (Book #12)
ONCE TRAPPED (Book #13)

MACKENZIE WHITE MYSTERY SERIES
BEFORE HE KILLS (Book #1)
BEFORE HE SEES (Book #2)
BEFORE HE COVETS (Book #3)
BEFORE HE TAKES (Book #4)
BEFORE HE NEEDS (Book #5)
BEFORE HE FEELS (Book #6)
BEFORE HE SINS (Book #7)
BEFORE HE HUNTS (Book #8)
BEFORE HE PREYS (Book #9)
BEFORE HE LONGS (Book #10)

AVERY BLACK MYSTERY SERIES
CAUSE TO KILL (Book #1)
CAUSE TO RUN (Book #2)
CAUSE TO HIDE (Book #3)
CAUSE TO FEAR (Book #4)
CAUSE TO SAVE (Book #5)
CAUSE TO DREAD (Book #6)

KERI LOCKE MYSTERY SERIES

PROLOGUE

Once, when she was a girl, Malory Thomas had come to this bridge with a boy. It was Halloween night and she was fourteen. They'd been looking down into the water one hundred and seventy-five feet below, looking for the ghosts of those who had committed suicide from the bridge. It was a ghost story that had circulated through their school, a story Malory had heard all her life. She let that boy kiss her that night but had pushed his hand away when it went up her shirt.

Now, thirteen years later, she thought of that innocent little gesture as she hung from that same bridge. It was called the Miller Moon Bridge and it was known for two things: being an awesome and secluded make-out spot for teens, and the number one suicide location in all of the county—maybe in the entire state of Virginia for all she knew.

In that moment, Malory Thomas did not care about the suicides, though. All she could think about was holding on to the edge of the bridge for dear life. She was clinging to the side with both hands, her fingers curled against the rugged wooden edge of it. Her right hand could not get a good grip because of the enormous bolt that went through the wood, affixing the strut along the side to the iron beams beneath it.

She tried to move her right hand to get a better grip but her hand was too sweaty. Moving it even an inch made her fear that she'd lose her grip completely and go falling all the way down to the water. And there wasn't much water there. All that awaited her below were jagged rocks and countless coins stupid kids had tossed off the side of the bridge to make pointless wishes.

She looked up to the rails along the edge of the bridge, old rusted trestle rails that looked ancient in the darkness of the midnight hour. She saw the shape of the man who had brought her here—a far cry from that brave teenage boy from thirteen years ago. No…this man was hateful and dark. She did not know him well but knew enough to now know for sure that something was wrong with him. He was sick, not right in the head, not well.

"Just let go," he told her. His voice was creepy, somewhere between Batman and a demon.

"Please," Malory said. "Please…help."

She didn't even care that she was naked, her bare rear end dangling from the edge of the Miller Moon Bridge. He had stripped her down and she was afraid he would rape her. But he hadn't. He'd only stared at her, run a hand along a few places, and then forced her to the edge of the bridge. She thought longingly of her clothes scattered on the wooden beams behind him, and had a sick sort of certainty that she would never wear them again.

With that certainty, her right hand cramped up as it tried to get used to the shape of the bolt beneath it. She cried out and felt all of her weight slip over to her left hand—her much weaker hand.

The man hunkered down, kneeling and looking at her. It was like he knew it was coming. Even before *she* knew the end was there, he knew it.

She could barely see his eyes in the darkness but she could see enough to tell that he was happy. Excited, maybe.

"It's okay," he said in that odd voice.

And as if the muscles in her fingers were obeying him, her right hand gave up. Malory felt a tightness all the way down through her forearm as her left hand tried to hold up her one hundred and forty pounds.

And just like that, she was no longer clinging to the bridge. She was falling. Her stomach did a cartwheel and her eyes seemed to tremble in their sockets as they tried to make sense of how fast the bridge was moving away from her.

For a moment, the wind rushing past her felt almost pleasant. She tried her best to focus on that as she scrambled for some kind of a prayer to utter in her final moments.

She only managed a few words—*Our Father, who art…*—and then Malory Thomas felt her life leave her body in a sharp and crushing blow as she slammed into the rocks below.

CHAPTER ONE

Mackenzie White had fallen into something of a routine. This did not sit particularly well with her because she was not the kind of woman who liked routine. If things stayed the same for too long, she felt they needed to be shaken up.

Only a few short days after finally bringing the long and miserable chapter of her father's murder to a close, she had come back to her apartment and realized that she and Ellington were now living together. She had no problem with this; she had been looking forward to it, actually. But there were nights during those first few weeks where she lost some sleep when she realized that her future now seemed stable. For the first time in a very long time, she had no real reason to chase hard after anything.

There had been her father's case, eating at her since she had first picked up a badge and a gun back in Nebraska. That was now solved. There had also been the uncertainty of where her relationship with Ellington was headed. They were now living together and almost sickeningly happy. She was excelling at work, gaining the respect of just about everyone within the FBI. Even McGrath seemed to have finally warmed up to her.

Things felt stationary. And for Mackenzie, she couldn't help but wonder: was this simply the calm before the storm? If her time as a detective in Nebraska and an agent with the FBI had taught her anything, it was that life had a way of snatching away any sort of comfort or security without much warning.

Still, the routine wasn't all bad. After Ellington had healed up from his wounds following the case that had brought her father's killer to justice, he was ordered to stay at home and rest. She tended to him as well as she could, discovering that she could be quite nurturing when she needed to be. After Ellington had fully recovered, her days were pretty standard. They were even enjoyable despite the horrid degree of domestication she felt.

She would go to work and stop by the firing range before returning home. When she got home, one of two things happened: either Ellington had already prepared dinner and they ate together like an old married couple, or they went directly to the bedroom, like a newly married couple.

All of this was going through her head as she and Ellington were settling down for bed. She was on her side of the bed, half-heartedly reading a book. Ellington was on his side of the bed, typing out an email about a case he had been working on. Seven weeks had passed since they'd closed the Nebraska case. Ellington had just started back to work and the routine of life was starting to become a stark reality for her.

"I'm going to ask you something," Mackenzie said. "And I want you to be honest."

"Okay," he said. He finished typing the sentence he was on and stopped, giving her his full attention.

"Did you ever see yourself in this kind of routine?" she asked.

"What routine?"

She shrugged, setting her book aside. "Being domesticated. Being tied down. Going to work, coming home, eating dinner, watching some TV, maybe having sex, then going to bed."

"If that's a routine, it seems pretty awesome. Maybe don't put *sometimes* in front of the sex part, though. Why do you ask? Does the routine bother you?"

"It doesn't *bother* me," she said. "It's just…it feels weird. It makes me feel like I'm not doing my part. Like I'm being lazy or passive about…well, about something I can't really put my finger on."

"You think this stems from the fact that you've finally wrapped your dad's case?" he asked.

"Probably."

There was something else, too. But it wasn't something she could tell him. She knew it was pretty difficult to emotionally hurt him but she didn't want to take the chance. The thought she kept to herself was that now that they had moved in and were happy and handling it like pros, it really only left one more step for them to take. It was not a step they had discussed and, honestly, not a step Mackenzie *wanted* to discuss.

Marriage. She was hoping Ellington wasn't there yet, either. Not that she didn't love him. But after that step…well, what else was there?

"Let me ask *you* something," Ellington said. "Are you happy? Like right now, in this very moment, knowing that tomorrow could very well be an exact duplicate of today. Are you happy?"

The answer was simple but still made her uneasy. "Yes," she said.

"Then why question it?"

4

She nodded. He had a good point and it honestly made her wonder if she was overcomplicating things. She'd be thirty in a few weeks, so maybe this was what a normal life was like. Once all of the demons and ghosts of the past had been buried, maybe *this* was what life was supposed to be like.

And that was fine, she supposed. But something about it felt stagnant and made her wonder if she'd *ever* allow herself to be happy.

CHAPTER TWO

Work was not helping the monotony of what Mackenzie was coming to think of as The Routine—capital *T* and capital *R*. In the nearly two months that had passed since the events in Nebraska, Mackenzie's case load had consisted of surveilling a group of men that were suspected of sex trafficking—spending her days sitting in a car or in abandoned buildings, listening to crude conversations that all turned out to be about nothing. She'd also worked alongside Yardley and Harrison on a case involving a suspected terrorist cell in Iowa—which had also turned out to be nothing.

The day following their tense conversation about happiness, Mackenzie found herself at her desk, researching one of the men she had been surveilling for sex trafficking. He was not part of a sex trafficking ring, but he was almost certainly involved in some sort of deranged prostitution set-up. It was hard to believe that she was qualified to carry a weapon, to hunt down murderers and save lives. She was starting to feel like a plastic employee, someone who served no real function.

Frustrated, she got up for a cup of coffee. She had never been one to wish anything bad upon anyone, but she was wondering if things in the country were really so good that her services might not be needed somewhere.

As she made her way to the small lobby-like area where the coffee machines were housed, she spotted Ellington putting the top on his own cup. He saw her coming and waited for her, though she could tell by his posture that he was in a hurry.

"I hope your day has been more exciting than mine," Mackenzie said.

"Maybe," he said. "Ask me again in half an hour. McGrath just called me up to his office."

"For what?" Mackenzie asked.

"No idea. He didn't call you, too?"

"No," she said, wondering what might be going on. While there had been no direct conversation about it with McGrath ever since the Nebraska case, she had just assumed that she and Ellington would remain partners. She wondered if maybe the department was finally deciding to separate them based on their romantic relationship. If so, she understood the decision but would not necessarily like it.

"I'm getting tired of riding my desk," she said as she poured her coffee. "Do me a favor and see if you can get me on whatever he sticks you on, too."

"Gladly," he said. "I'll keep you posted."

She walked back to her office, wondering if this small break in normalcy might be the one thing she had been waiting for—the crack that would start to chip away at the foundation of routine she'd been feeling. It wasn't often that McGrath summoned just one of them to his office—not recently, anyway. It made her wonder if she was perhaps under some kind of review that she didn't know about. Was McGrath digging harder into the last case in Nebraska to make sure she had done everything by the book? If that was the case then she might be in some hot water because she had most definitely *not* done everything by the book.

Sadly, wondering what the meeting between Ellington and McGrath was about was the most interesting thing that had happened in the last week or so. It was what occupied her mind as she sat back down in front of her computer, once again feeling like nothing more than another cog in the wheel.

***

She heard footsteps fifteen minutes later. This was nothing new; she worked with her office door open and saw people walking back and forth up and down the hallway all day. But this was different. This sounded like several pairs of footsteps all walking in unison. There was also a sense of quiet—a hushed tension like the atmosphere just before a violent summer thunderstorm.

Curious, Mackenzie looked up from her laptop. As the footsteps got louder, she saw Ellington. He quickly glanced through the doorway, his face tight with an emotion she couldn't quite place. He was carrying a box in his hands while two security guards followed closely behind him.

What the hell?

Mackenzie jumped up from her desk and ran into the hall. Just as she was coming around the corner, Ellington and the two guards were getting on the elevator. The doors slid closed and once again, Mackenzie just barely caught sight of that tense expression on his face.

He's been fired, she thought. The idea was absolutely ridiculous as far as she was concerned, but that's what it seemed like.

She ran to the stairwell, pushing the door open quickly and heading down. She took the steps two at a time, hoping to make it out before Ellington and the guards did. She rushed down the three flights of stairs, coming out along the side of the building directly next to the parking garage.

She came out of the door at the same time Ellington and the guards exited the building. Mackenzie rushed across the lawn to cut them off. The guards looked on edge when they saw her coming, one of them stopping for a moment and facing her as if she might actually be a threat.

"What is it?" she asked over the guard, looking at Ellington.

He shook his head. "Not right now," he said. "Just…let it go for now."

"What's going on?" she asked. "The guards…the box…have you been fired? What the hell happened?"

He shook his head again. There was nothing mean or dismissive about it. She figured it was the best he could do in the situation. Maybe something had occurred that he *couldn't* talk about. And Ellington, loyal to a fault, would not speak if he had been asked to stay quiet.

She hated to do it, but she didn't press him any farther. If she wanted direct answers, there was only one place to get them. With that in mind, she ran back into the building. This time she took the elevator, taking it back to the third floor and wasting no time marching down the hall toward McGrath's office.

She didn't bother checking in with his secretary as she headed for his door. She heard the woman call her name, trying to stop her, but Mackenzie went in. She did not knock, just walked right into the office.

McGrath was at his desk, clearly not at all surprised that she was there. He turned toward her and the calmness on his face infuriated her.

"Just remain calm, Agent White," he said.

"What happened?" she asked. "Why did I just see Ellington escorted from the building with a box of his personal belongings?"

"Because he's been released from duty."

The simplicity of the statement did not make it any easier to hear. Part of her was still wondering if there had been some huge mistake. Or if this was all some huge elaborate joke.

"For what?"

8

She then saw something she had never seen before: McGrath looking away, clearly uncomfortable. "It's a private matter," he said. "I understand the relationship between the two of you, but this is information I can legally not divulge due to the nature of the situation."

In all of her time working under McGrath, she had never heard so much legalistic bullshit come out of his mouth at one time. She managed to quash her anger. After all, this was not about her. There was apparently something going on with Ellington that she knew nothing about.

"Is everything okay?" she asked. "Can you tell me *that* much?"

"That's not for me to answer, I'm afraid," McGrath said. "Now, if you'll excuse me, I'm actually pretty busy."

Mackenzie gave a little nod and backed out of the office, closing the door behind her. The secretary behind her own desk gave her a nasty look that Mackenzie ignored completely. She walked back to her office and checked her mail to reconfirm that the remainder of her day was a slow void of nothing.

She then hurried out of the building, doing her best not to look like something was troubling her. The last thing she needed was for half of the building to be aware that Ellington was gone and that she was rushing out behind him. She'd finally managed to overcome the prying eyes and almost legendary rumors of her past within the workplace and she'd be damned if she'd create another reason for the cycle to start all over.

***

She felt confident that Ellington had simply gone back to their apartment. When she'd first met him, he'd been the kind of man who would maybe go directly to a bar in an attempt to drown his sorrows. But he had changed in the last year or so—just as she had. She supposed they owed that to each other. It was a thought she kept in mind as she opened the door to her apartment (*their* apartment, she reminded herself), hoping to find him inside.

Sure enough, she found him in the small second bedroom they used as an office. He was unpacking the things he'd had in his box, tossing them haphazardly onto the desk they shared. He looked up when he saw her but then quickly looked away.

"Sorry," he said with his head turned. "You're not exactly catching me on my best day."

She approached him but resisted placing a hand on his shoulder or an arm around his back. She had never seen him so out of sorts.

9

It alarmed her a bit but, more than anything, made her want to see what she could do to help.

"What happened?" she asked.

"Seems pretty obvious, doesn't it?" he asked. "I've been suspended indefinitely."

"What the hell for?" She again thought of McGrath and how uncomfortable he had looked when she had posed this same question to him.

He finally turned to her again and when he did, she could see embarrassment on his face. When he answered her, his voice was trembling.

"Sexual harassment."

For a moment, the words didn't make much sense. She waited for him to smile at her and tell her that he was just kidding, but that never happened. Instead, his eyes locked on hers, waiting for her reaction.

"What?" she asked. "When was this?"

"About three years ago," he said. "But the woman just came forward with the allegations three days ago."

"And is the allegation a valid one?" she asked.

He nodded, taking a seat at the desk. "Mackenzie, I'm sorry. I was a different guy back then, you know?"

She was angry for a moment, but she wasn't sure at who: Ellington or the woman. "What sort of harassment?" she asked.

"I was training this younger agent three years ago," he said. "She was doing really well so one night, a few agents took her out to celebrate. We all had a few drinks and she and I were the last ones left. At the time, the thought of hitting on her had never crossed my mind. But I went to the restroom and when I came out, she was right there waiting for me. She kissed me and it got heated. She pulled away—maybe realizing it was a mistake. And then I tried to go back in. I'd like to think that had I not been drinking, her pulling away would have been the end of it. But I didn't stop. I tried to kiss her again and didn't realize she wasn't returning it until she pushed me away. She pushed me off of her and just stared me down. I told her I was sorry—and I meant it—but she just stormed out. And that was it. A sad little encounter between bathrooms. No one forced themselves on anyone else and there was no groping or other misconduct. The next day when I got to work, she had asked to be transferred to another agent. Within two months, she was gone, transferred to Seattle, I think."

"And why is she bringing this up now?" Mackenzie asked.

"Because it's the popular thing to do these days," Ellington snapped. He then shook his head and sighed. "Sorry. That was a shitty thing to say."

"Yes, it was. Are you telling me the whole story? Is that all that happened?"

"That's it," he said. "I swear it."

"You were married, right? When it happened?"

He nodded. "It's not one of my prouder moments."

Mackenzie thought of the first time she'd spent any significant time with Ellington. It had been during the Scarecrow Killer case in Nebraska. She had basically thrown herself at him while she had been in the midst of her own personal dramas. She could tell that he had been interested but in the end, he had declined her advances.

She wondered how heavily the encounter with this woman had been weighing on his mind during that night when she'd offered herself to him.

"How long is the suspension?" she asked.

He shrugged. "It depends. If she decides not to make too big of a stink about it, it could be as little as a month. But if it goes big, it could be much longer. In the end, it could lead to a total termination."

Mackenzie turned away this time. She couldn't help but feel a little selfish. Sure, she was upset that a man she cared very deeply about was going through something like this, but at the root of it all, she was more concerned with losing her partner. She hated that her priorities were so skewed, but that's the way she felt in that moment. That and an intense jealousy that she *loathed*. She was not the jealous type...so why was she so jealous of the woman who had reported the so-called harassment? She'd never thought of Ellington's wife with any hints of jealousy, so why this woman?

Because she's causing everything to change, she thought. *That boring little routine I was falling into and growing comfortable with is starting to crumble.*

"What are you thinking?" Ellington asked.

Mackenzie shook her head and looked at her watch. It was only one in the afternoon. Pretty soon, her absence would be noticed at work.

"I'm thinking I need to get back to work," she said. And with that, she turned away from him again and walked out of the room.

"Mackenzie," Ellington called out. "Hold on."

"It's okay," she called out to him. "I'll see you in a little bit."

She left without a goodbye, a kiss, or a hug. Because even though she had said it, things were *not* okay.

If things were okay, she wouldn't be fighting back tears that seemed to have come out of nowhere. If things were okay, she wouldn't still be trying to push away an anger that kept trying to claw its way up, telling her that she was a fool to think that life would be okay now, that she was finally due a normal life where the haunts of her past didn't influence everything.

By the time she reached her car, she had managed to bring the tears to a stop. Her cell phone rang, Ellington's name popping up. She ignored it, started the car, and headed back to work.

CHAPTER THREE

Work only provided distance for a few more hours. Even when Mackenzie checked in with Harrison to make sure he didn't need assistance on the small wiring fraud case he was working on, she was out of the building by six. When she arrived back at the apartment at 6:20, she found Ellington behind the stove. He didn't cook often and when he did, it was usually because he had idle hands and nothing better to do.

"Hey," he said, looking up from a pot of what looked like some sort of stir-fry.

"Hey," she said in return, setting her laptop bag down on the couch and walking into the kitchen. "Sorry I left the way I did earlier."

"No need to apologize," he said.

"Of course there is. It was immature. And if I'm being honest, I don't know why it upsets me so much. I'm more worried about losing you as a partner than I am about what this might do to your professional record. How messed up is that?"

He shrugged. "It makes sense."

"It *should* but it doesn't," she said. "I can't think about you kissing another woman, especially not in a way like that. Even if you *were* drunk and even if she *did* initiate things, I can't see you like that. And it makes me want to kill that woman, you know?"

"I'm sorry as hell," he said. "It's one of those things in life I wish I could take back. One of those things I thought was in the past and I was done with."

Mackenzie walked up behind him and hesitantly wrapped her arms around his waist. "Are you okay?" she asked.

"Just mad. And embarrassed."

Part of Mackenzie feared that he was being dishonest with her. There was something in his posture, something about the way he couldn't quite look at her when he talked about it. She wanted to think it was simply because it was not easy to be accused of something like this, to be reminded of something stupid you'd done in your past.

Honestly, she wasn't sure what to believe. Ever since she'd seen him walking by her office door with the box in his hands, her thoughts toward him were mixed up and confused.

She was about to offer to help with dinner, hoping some normalcy might help them to get back on track. But before the words could come out of her mouth, her cell phone rang. She was surprised and a little worried to see that it was from McGrath.

"Sorry," she said to Ellington, showing him the display. "I should probably take this."

"He probably wants to ask if you've ever felt sexually harassed by me," he said snidely.

"He already had the chance earlier today," she said before stepping away from the sizzling noises of the kitchen to answer the phone.

"This is White," she said, speaking directly and almost mechanically, as she tended to do when answering a call from McGrath.

"White," he said. "Are you home yet?"

"Yes sir."

"I need you to come back out. I need to speak with you in private. I'll be in the parking garage. Level Two, Row D."

"Sir, is this about Ellington?"

"Just meet me there, White. Get there as quickly as you can."

He ended the call with that, leaving Mackenzie holding a dead line in her hand. She pocketed it slowly, looking back toward Ellington. He was removing the pan from the stove, heading to the table in the little dining area.

"I have to grab some to go," she said.

"Damn. Is it about me?"

"He wouldn't say," Mackenzie said. "But I don't think so. This is something different. He's being really secretive."

She wasn't sure why, but she left out the instructions to meet him in the parking garage. If she was being honest with herself, something about that didn't sit well with her. Still, she grabbed a bowl from the cabinets, spooned some of Ellington's dinner into it, and gave him a kiss on the cheek. Both of them could tell that it felt mechanical and forced.

"Keep me posted," Ellington said. "And let me know if you need anything."

"Of course," she said.

Realizing she hadn't even yet removed her holster and Glock, she headed directly for the door. And it wasn't until she was back out into the hallway and heading for her car that she realized that she was actually quite relieved to have been called away.

***

She had to admit that it felt a little cliché to be slowly creeping along Level 2 of the parking garage across from headquarters. Meeting in parking garages was the stuff of bad TV cop dramas. And in those dramas, shady parking garage meetings usually led to drama of some kind or another.

She spotted McGrath's car and parked her own car a few spaces away. She locked up and strolled down to where McGrath was waiting. Without any formal invitation to do so, she walked to the passenger side door, opened it, and climbed in.

"Okay," she said. "The secrecy is killing me. What's wrong?"

"Nothing is wrong per se," McGrath said. "But we've got a case about an hour or so away in a little town called Kingsville. You know it?"

"Heard of it, but never been there."

"It's about as rural as you can imagine, tucked away in the last stretch of backwoods before all of the commotion and interstates of DC take over," McGrath said. "But it actually might not be a case at all. That's what I need you to go figure out."

"Okay," she said. "But why couldn't we have this meeting in your office?"

"Because the victim is the deputy director's nephew. Twenty-two years old. It looks like someone tossed him from a bridge. The local PD in Kingsville say it's probably just a suicide, but Deputy Director Wilmoth wants to make sure."

"Does he have any reason to believe it was a murder?" she asked.

"Well, it's the second body that's been found at the bottom of that bridge in the last four days. It probably *is* a suicide if you want my opinion. But I had the order passed down to me about an hour ago, straight from Director Wilmoth. He wants to know for sure. He also wants to be informed as soon as possible *and* he wants it kept quiet. Hence the request to meet with me here rather than in my office. If anyone saw you and I meeting after hours, they'd assume it was about what is going on with Ellington or that I had you on some special assignment."

"So...go to Kingsville, figure out if this was a suicide or murder, and then report back?"

"Yes. And because of recent events with Ellington, you'll be flying solo. Which shouldn't be an issue as I expect you'll be back late tonight with news that it was a suicide."

"Understood. When do I leave?"

"Now," he said. "No time like the present, right?"

CHAPTER FOUR

Mackenzie discovered that McGrath had not been exaggerating when he had described Kingsville, Virginia, as *backwoods*. It was a little town that, in terms of identity, was tucked somewhere between *Deliverance* and *Amityville*. It had a creepy rural vibe to it but with the small-town rustic charm of what most people likely expected of smaller southern towns.

Night had completely fallen by the time she arrived at the crime scene. The bridge came into view slowly as she carefully drove her car down a thin gravel road. The road itself was not a state-maintained road yet was also not completely closed off to the public. However, when she closed in to less than fifty yards of the bridge, she saw that the Kingsville PD had put up a row of sawhorses to keep anyone from going any farther.

She parked alongside a few local police cars and then stepped out into the night. A few spotlights had been set up, all shining down the steep bank to the right side of the bridge. As she approached the drop-off, a young-looking policeman stepped out of one of the cars.

"You Agent White?" the man asked, his southern accent cutting into her like a razor.

"I am," she answered.

"Okay. You might find it easier to walk across the bridge and go down the other side of the embankment. This side is steep as hell."

Thankful for the tip, Mackenzie walked across the bridge. She took out her little Maglite and inspected the area as she crossed. The bridge was quite old, surely having long ago been shut down for any sort of practical use. She knew that there were many bridges scattered across Virginia and West Virginia that were very similar to this one. This bridge, called Miller Moon Bridge according to the basic research she'd managed to do on Google during traffic-light stops along the way, had been standing since 1910 and shut down for public use in 1969. And while that was the only information she'd been able to get on the location, her current investigation was pulling out more details.

There wasn't much graffiti along the bridge, but the amount of litter was noticeable. Beer bottles, soda cans, and empty bags of chips were tossed to the edges of the bridge, pushed against the metal edging that supported the iron rails. The bridge wasn't very long at all; it was around seventy-five yards, just long enough to span over the steep embankments and the river below. It felt sturdy under her feet but the very structure of it was almost feeble in a way. She was very aware that she was walking on wooden boards and support beams nearly two hundred feet in the air.

She made her way to the end of the bridge, finding that the police officer had been right. The land was much more manageable on this other side. With the help of the Maglite, she saw a beaten path that wound through the high grass. The embankment went down at close to a ninety-degree angle but there were patches of ground and rocks jutting out here and there that made the descent quite easy.

"Hold on a minute," a man's voice said from below. Mackenzie glanced forward, toward the glare of the spotlights, and saw a shadow emerging and coming her way. "Who's there?" the man asked.

"Mackenzie White, FBI," she said, reaching for her ID.

The shadow's owner came into view moments later. He was an older man with a huge bushy beard. He was wearing a police uniform, the badge over his breast indicating that he was Kingsville's sheriff. Behind him, she could see the figures of four other officers. One of them was taking pictures and moving slowly in the shadows.

"Oh, wow," he said. "That was quick." He waited for Mackenzie to draw closer and then extended his hand. He gave her a hearty handshake and said, "I'm Sheriff Tate. Good to meet you."

"Likewise," Mackenzie said as she reached the end of the embankment and found herself on flat land.

She took a moment to take in the scene, expertly illuminated by the spotlights that had been set up along the sides of the embankment. The first thing Mackenzie noticed was that the river wasn't much of a river at all—not in the location beneath Miller Moon Bridge, anyway. There were what looked like a few meandering puddles of stagnant water hugging the sides and sharp edges of rocks and large boulders that took up the area the river should have passed through.

One of the boulders among the rubble was massive, easily the size of two cars. Splayed out on top of this boulder was a body. The right arm was clearly broken, bent impossibly beneath the remainder of the body. A stream of blood was trailing down the boulder, mostly dried but still wet enough to seem as if it was still flowing.

"Hell of a sight, ain't it?" Tate asked, standing beside her.

"Yes, it is. What can you tell me for sure at the moment?"

"Well, the victim is a twenty-two-year-old male. Kenny Skinner. As I understand it, he's related to someone higher up on your ladder."

"Yes. The nephew of the FBI's deputy director. How many men out here currently know that?"

"Just me and my deputy," Tate said. "We already spoke with your pals in Washington. We know this needs to be kept quiet."

"Thanks," Mackenzie said. "I understand there was another body discovered here a few days ago?"

"Three mornings ago, yeah," Tate said. "A woman named Malory Thomas."

"Any signs of foul play?"

"Well, she was naked. And her clothes were found up there on the bridge. Other than that, there was nothing. It was assumed to be just another suicide."

"You get many of those around here?"

"Yeah," Tate said with a nervous smile. "You could say that. Three years ago, six people killed themselves by jumping off of this fucking bridge. It was some kind of record per location for the state of Virginia. The year after that, there were three. Last year, it was five."

"Were they all locals?" Mackenzie asked.

"No. Out of those fourteen people, only four living within a fifty-mile radius."

"And to your knowledge, is there maybe some sort of urban legend or reasoning behind these people taking their lives off of this bridge?"

"There's ghost stories, sure," Tate said. "But there's a ghost story tied to just about every decommissioned bridge in the country. I don't know. I blame these screwed up generation gaps. Kids these days get their feelings hurt and think offing themselves is the answer. It's pretty sad."

"How about homicides?" Mackenzie asked. "What's the rate like in Kingsville?"

"There were two last year. And so far, only one this year. It's a quiet town. Everyone knows everyone else and if you don't like someone, you just stay away from them. Why do you ask? You leaning towards murder for this one?"

"I don't know yet," Mackenzie said. "Two bodies in the span of four days, at the same location. I think it's worth looking into. Do you happen to know if Kenny Skinner and Malory Thomas knew one another?"

"Probably. But I don't know how well. Like I said…everyone knows everyone in Kingsville. But if you're asking if maybe Kenny killed himself because Malory did, I doubt it. There's a five-year difference in age and they didn't really hang with the same crowds from what I know."

"Mind if I have a look?" Mackenzie asked.

"Be my guest," Tate said, instantly walking away from her to join the other officers who were scouring the scene.

Mackenzie approached the boulder and the body of Kenny Skinner apprehensively. The closer she got to the body, the more aware she became of just how much damage had been done. She'd seen some pretty grisly things in her line of work, but this was among the worst.

The stream of blood was coming from an area where it appeared Kenny's head had smashed against the rock. She didn't bother examining it closely because the black and red illuminated in the spotlights wasn't something she wanted popping back into her head later in the night. The massive facture in the back of his head affected the rest of the skull, distorting the facial features. She also saw where his chest and stomach looked as if they had been puffed out from within.

She did her best to look past all of this, checking over Kenny's clothes and exposed skin for any signs of foul play. In the harsh yet inefficient beam of the spotlights, it was hard to be sure but after several minutes, Mackenzie could find nothing. When she stepped away, she felt herself start to relax. Apparently, she'd been tensed up while observing the body.

She went back to Sheriff Tate, who was speaking with another officer. They sounded as if they were making plans about notifying the family.

"Sheriff, do you think you could have someone pull the records for me on those fourteen suicides over the last three years?"

"Yeah, I can do that. I'll make a call here in a second and make sure they're waiting for you at the station. And you know…there's someone you might want to call. There's a lady in town, works out of her home as a psychiatrist and special needs teacher. She's been on my ass for the last year or so about how all of the suicides in Kingsville can't *just* be suicides. She might be able to offer something you might not find in the reports."

"That would be great."

"I'll have someone include her information with the reports. You good here?"

"For now, yes. Could I please have your number for easier contact?"

"Sure. But the damned thing is glitchy. Need to upgrade. Should have done it about five months back. So if you call me and it goes to voicemail right away, I'm not ignoring you. I'll call you right back. Some stupid thing with the phone. I hate cell phones anyway."

After his rant on modern technology, Tate gave her his cell number and she saved it into her phone.

"I'll see you around," Tate said. "For now, the coroner is on the way. I'll be damn glad when we can move this body."

It seemed like an insensitive thing to say but when Mackenzie looked back at it and saw the gore and broken state of the body, she couldn't help but agree.

CHAPTER FIVE

It was 10:10 when she walked into the police station. The place was absolutely dead, the only movement coming from a bored-looking woman sitting behind a desk—what Mackenzie assumed served as dispatch at the Kingsville Police Department—and two officers talking animatedly about politics in a hallway behind the dispatch desk.

Despite the lackluster feel of the place, it was apparently very well run. The woman at the dispatch desk had already copied all of the records Sheriff Tate had mentioned and had them waiting in a file folder when Mackenzie arrived. Mackenzie thanked her and then asked for a motel recommendation in the area. As it turned out, Kingsville only had a single motel, less than two miles away from the police department.

Ten minutes later, Mackenzie was unlocking the door to her room at a Motel 6. She'd certainly stayed in worse places during her tenure with the bureau, but it wasn't likely to get any glowing Yelp or Google reviews. She paid little attention to the lacking state of the room, setting the files down on the little table by the single bed and wasting no time in diving into them.

She took some notes of her own while she read through the files. The first and perhaps most alarming thing she discovered was that of the fourteen suicides that had occurred in the last three years, eleven of them had been from the Miller Moon Bridge. The other three included two gun-related suicides and a single hanging from an attic beam.

Mackenzie knew enough about small towns to understand the allure of a rural marker like the Miller Moon Bridge. The history and the overall neglected creepiness of it was appealing, especially to teens. And, as the records in front of her showed, six of the fourteen suicides had been under twenty-one years of age.

She pored over the records; while they weren't as explicitly detailed as she would have liked, they were above par for what she had seen from most small-town police departments. She jotted down note after note, coming up with a comprehensive list of details to help her better get to the bottom of the multiple deaths that were linked to the Miller Moon Bridge. After an hour or so, she had enough to base a few rough opinions.

First, of the fourteen suicides, exactly half had left notes. The notes made it clear that they had made the decision to end their lives. Each record had a photocopy of the letter and all of them expressed regret of some form or another. They told loved ones they cherished them and expressed pains that they could not overcome.

The other seven could almost be looked at as typical suspected murder cases: bodies discovered out of nowhere, in rough shape. One of the suicides, a seventeen-year-old female, had shown evidence of recent sexual activity. When the DNA of her partner had been found on and in her body, he had provided evidence in the form of text messages that she had come to his house, they'd had sex, and then she'd left. And from the way it looked, she had launched herself off of the Miller Moon Bridge about three hours later.

The only case out of the fourteen that she could see that would have warranted any sort of closer look was the sad and unfortunate suicide of a sixteen-year-old male. When he had been discovered on those bloodied rocks beneath the bridge, there had been bruises on his chest and arms that did not line up with any of the injuries he had suffered from the fall itself. Within a few days, police had discovered that the boy had been routinely beaten by an alcoholic father who, sadly enough, attempted suicide three days after the discovery of his son's body.

Mackenzie finished off the research session with the freshly put together file on Malory Thomas. Her case stood out a bit from the others because she had been nude. The report showed that her clothes had been found in a neat pile on the bridge. There had been so sign of abuse, recent sexual activity, or foul play. For some reason or another, it simply seemed that Malory Thomas had decided to take that leap in her birthday suit.

That seems odd, though, Mackenzie thought. *Out of place, even. If you're going to kill yourself, why would you want yourself exposed like that when your body is found?*

She pondered it for a moment and then remembered the psychiatrist Sheriff Tate had mentioned. Of course, now that it was nearly midnight, it was too late to call.

Midnight, she thought. She looked to her phone, surprised that Ellington had not tried reaching out. She supposed he was playing it smart—not wanting to bother her until he thought she was in a good place. And honestly, she wasn't sure what sort of place she was in.

So he'd made a mistake in his life long before he knew her...why the hell should she be so upset about that?

She wasn't sure. But she knew that she *was*...and in that moment, that was really all that mattered.

Before turning in for bed, she looked at the business card the woman at the station had placed in the file. It was the name, number, and email address of the local psychiatrist, Dr. Jan Haggerty. Wanting to be as prepared as possible, Mackenzie fired off an email, letting Dr. Haggerty know that she was in town, why she was there, and requesting a meeting as early as possible. Mackenzie figured if she had not heard from Haggerty by nine tomorrow morning, she'd go ahead and place a call.

Before turning out the lights, she thought about calling Ellington, just to check on him. She knew him well enough; he was probably having a pity party for himself, likely downing several beers with plans of passing out on the couch.

Thinking of him in that state made the decision much easier for her. She turned out the lights and, in the darkness, started to feel like she might be in a town that was darker than others. The kind of town that hid some ugly scars, forever in the dark not because of the rural setting but because of a certain blemish on a gravel road about six miles from where she currently rested her head. And although she did her best to clear her thoughts, she fell asleep with images of teenagers falling to their deaths from the top of Miller Moon Bridge.

CHAPTER SIX

She was stirred awake by the ringing of her cell phone. The bedside clock told her that it was 6:40 as she reached for it. She saw McGrath's name on the display, had just enough time to wish it were Ellington instead, and then answered it.

"This is Agent White."

"White, where are we on this case with Director Wilmoth's nephew?"

"Well, right now it seems like a clear-cut suicide. If it plays out the way I think it will, I should be back in DC this afternoon."

"No foul play at all?"

"Not that I can see. If you don't mind my asking…is Director Wilmoth *looking* for foul play?"

"No. But let's be real…a suicide in the family for a man of his position isn't going to look good. He just wants the details before the public gets them."

"Roger that."

"White, did I wake you?" he asked gruffly.

"Of course not, sir."

"Keep me in the loop on this," he said and then ended the call.

A hell of a way to wake up, Mackenzie thought as she got out of bed. She went to the shower and when she was done, a towel wrapped around her, she walked out of the bathroom to the sound of her phone going off yet again.

She did not recognize the number, so she picked it up right away. With her hair still wet, she answered: "This is Agent White."

"Agent White, this is Jan Haggerty," said a somber-sounding voice. "I just finished reading your email."

"Thanks for getting back to me so soon," Mackenzie said. "I know it's asking a lot for someone in your profession, but is there any way you and I could meet for a chat sometime today?"

"That's not a problem at all," Haggerty said. "My office is out of my home and my first appointment isn't until nine thirty this morning. If you give me half an hour or so to prepare for my day, I can see you this morning. I'll put on some coffee."

"Sounds great," Mackenzie said.

Haggerty gave Mackenzie her address and they ended the call. With half an hour to spare, Mackenzie decided she should do the grown-up thing and give Ellington a call. It would do neither of them any good to hide away from the issue at hand and just hope the other simply forgot about it or was able to sweep it under the rug.

When he answered the call, he sounded tired. Mackenzie assumed she had woken him up, which wasn't all that surprising since he tended to sleep in on the days he had off. But she was pretty sure she also detected some hopefulness in his voice.

"Hey," he said.

"Good morning," she said. "How are you?"

"I don't know," he said almost right away. "Out of sorts would be the best way to describe it. But I'll survive. The more I think about it, the more sure I am that this will all blow over. I'll have a little blemish on my professional record, but as long as I can return back to work, I think I'll manage. How about you? How's your super-top-secret case?"

"Pretty much over, I think," she said. When she had called him last night on her way to Kingsville, she had not shared too much information with him, just letting him know that it was not a case that would place her in any danger. She remained careful not to spill too much information now. It sometimes tended to happen among agents when a case was closed or close to being closed.

"Good," he said. "Because I don't like how things ended with us when you left. I don't...well, I don't know what I need to apologize for. But I still feel like I've done you a disservice in all of this."

"It is what it is," Mackenzie said, hating the sound of such a cliché coming out of her mouth. "I should be back by tonight. We can talk about it then."

"Sounds good. Be careful."

"You, too," she said with a forced chuckle.

They ended the call and while she felt a bit better having spoken to him, she couldn't deny the tension she still felt. She didn't allow herself time to dwell on it, though. She headed out into Kingsville in search of a bite to eat to pass the time before heading to Dr. Haggerty's house.

***

Dr. Haggerty lived alone in a two-story Colonial-style house. It sat in the center of a beautiful front yard. A thick group of elms and

26

oaks in the backyard hovered behind the house like nature's own form of drop shadow. Dr. Haggerty met Mackenzie at the front door with a smile and the scent of freshly brewed strong coffee right behind her. She looked to be in her late fifties, with a head of hair that was still managing to maintain most of its chestnut brown. Her eyes took Mackenzie in from behind a small set of glasses. When she invited Mackenzie inside, she gestured through the front door with rail-thin arms and a voice that was little more than a whisper.

"Thanks again for meeting with me," Mackenzie said. "I know it was short notice."

"No worries at all," she said. "Between you and me, I hope we can come up with enough cause for me to have Sheriff Tate put a bug in the county's ear to demolish that damn bridge."

Haggerty poured Mackenzie a cup of coffee and the two women sat down at the small table in a quaint breakfast nook just off the kitchen. A window by the side of the table looked out to those oaks and elms in the backyard.

"I assume you've been informed about the news from yesterday afternoon?" Mackenzie asked.

"I have," Haggerty said. "Kenny Skinner. Twenty-two years old, right?"

Mackenzie nodded as she sipped from her coffee. "And Malory Thomas several days before that. Now…can you tell me why you've been on the sheriff's case about the bridge?"

"Well, Kingsville has very little to offer. And while no one living in a small town wants to admit it, there is never anything for a small town to offer teens and young adults. And when that happens, these morbid landmarks like the Miller Moon Bridge become iconic. If you look back at the town records, people were ending their lives on that bridge as early as 1956, when it was still in use. Young kids these days are exposed to so much negativity and self-esteem issues that something as iconic as that bridge can become so much more. Kids looking for a way out of the town go to the extremes and it's no longer about escaping the town…it's about escaping life."

"So you think that the bridge gives suicidal kids an easy way out?"

"Not an easy way out," Haggerty said. "It's almost like a beacon for them. And those that have jumped off of the bridge before them have just led the way. That bridge isn't even really a bridge anymore. It's a suicide platform."

"Last night, Sheriff Tate also said that you find it hard to believe that these suicides can't all *just* be suicides. Can you elaborate on that?"

"Yes...and I believe I can use Kenny Skinner as an example. Kenny was a popular guy. Between you and me, he likely wasn't going to amount to anything extraordinary. He'd probably be perfectly fine to ride out the rest of his life here, working at the Kingsville Tire and Tractor Supply. But he had a good life here, you know? From what I know, he was something of a ladies' man and in a town like this—hell, in a *county* like this—that pretty much guarantees some fun weekends. I personally spoke with Kenny within the last month or so when I ran over a nail. He patched it up for me. He was polite, laughing, a well-mannered guy. I find it very hard to believe he killed himself in such a way. And if you go back through the list of people that have jumped off of that bridge in the last three years, there are at least one or two more that I find very fishy...people that I would have never pegged for suicide."

"So you feel that there's foul play involved?" Mackenzie asked.

Haggerty took a moment before she answered. "It's a suspicion I have, but I would not be comfortable saying as much with absolute certainty."

"And I assume this feeling is based on your professional opinion and not just someone saddened by so many suicides in your small hometown?" Mackenzie asked.

"That's correct," Haggerty said, but she seemed almost a little offended at the nature of the question.

"By any chance, did you ever see Kenny Skinner or Malory Thomas as clients?"

"No. And none of the other victims from as far back as 1996."

"So you *have* met with at least one of the suicides from the bridge?"

"Yes, on one occasion. And with that one, I saw it coming. I did everything I could to convince the family that she needed help. But by the time I could even manage to get them to consider it, she jumped right off that bridge. You see...in this town, the Miller Moon Bridge is synonymous with suicide. And that's why I'd really like for the county to tear it down."

"Because you feel that it basically calls to anyone with suicidal thoughts?"

"Exactly."

Mackenzie sensed that the conversation was basically over. And that was fine with her. She could tell straightaway that Dr.

Haggerty was not the type to exaggerate something just to make sure her voice was heard. Although she had tried to downplay it out of a fear of being wrong, Mackenzie was pretty sure Haggerty strongly believed that at least a few of the cases weren't suicides.

And that little bit of skepticism was all Mackenzie needed. If there was even the slightest chance that either of these last two bodies were murders and not suicides, she wanted to know for certain before heading back to DC.

She finished off her coffee, thanked Dr. Haggerty for her time, and then headed back outside. On the way to her car, she looked out to the forest that bordered most of Kingsville. She looked to the west, where the Miller Moon Bridge sat tucked away down a series of back roads and one gravel road that seemed to indicate all travelers were coming to the end of something.

As she thought about those bloodstained rocks at the bottom of the bridge, the comparison sent a small shiver through Mackenzie's heart.

She pushed it away, starting the engine and pulling out her cell phone. If she was going to get a definitive answer on any of this, she needed to treat it as if it *was* murder case. And with that mindset, she supposed she needed to start speaking to the family members of the recently deceased.

CHAPTER SEVEN

Before visiting the family of Kenny Skinner, Mackenzie called to get explicit permission from McGrath. His response had been short, clear, and to the point: *I don't care if you have to talk to someone on the fucking Little League baseball team, just get it figured out.*

That confirmation pushed her toward the residence of Pam and Vincent Skinner. The way McGrath explained it, Pam Skinner was formerly Pam Wilmoth. An older sister to Deputy Director Wilmoth, she worked from home as a proposal specialist for an environmental agency. As for Vincent Skinner, he just happened to be the owner of Kingsville Tire and Tractor Supply, having provided a job for his son since Kenny was fifteen.

When Mackenzie knocked on the door, neither of the Skinners greeted her. Instead, it was the pastor of Kingsville Presbyterian Church. When Mackenzie showed him her ID and told him why she was there, he let her in and asked her to wait in the foyer. The Skinner family lived in a nice house on a corner lot in what she assumed would be considered Kingsville's downtown area. She smelled something cooking, wafting down from a long hallway. Elsewhere in the house, she could hear the ringing of a cell phone. She also heard the muffled voice of the pastor, letting Pam and Vincent Skinner know that there was a lady from the FBI there to ask a few questions about Kenny.

It took a few minutes but Pam Skinner eventually came to meet her. The woman was red-faced from crying and looked as if she had not slept a wink the night before. "Are you Agent White?" she asked.

"I am."

"Thanks for coming," Pam said. "My brother told me you'd be coming by at some point."

"If it's too soon, I can—"

"No, no, I want to get it out now," she said.

"Is your husband at home?"

"He's elected to stay in the living room with our pastor. Vincent took this incredibly hard. He fainted twice last night and goes through these little moments where he just refuses to believe it's happened and—"

As if out of nowhere, a huge sob escaped Pam's throat and she leaned against the wall. She hitched her breath and swallowed down what Mackenzie was sure was grief that needed to come out.

"Mrs. Skinner…I can come back later."

"No. Now, please. I've had to stay strong all night for Vincent. I can manage a few more minutes for you. Just…come on to the kitchen."

Mackenzie followed Pam Skinner down the hallway and toward the kitchen, where Mackenzie started to recognize the smell she'd noticed earlier. Apparently, Pam had put some cinnamon rolls in the oven, perhaps in an effort to continue putting off her sorrow for her husband. Pam checked on them half-heartedly as Mackenzie settled down at a stool by the kitchen bar.

"I spoke with Dr. Haggerty this morning," Mackenzie said. "She's been lobbying to have the Miller Moon Bridge torn down. Your son's name came up. She said she finds it very hard to believe that Kenny would have taken his own life."

Pan nodded emphatically. "She's absolutely right. Kenny would have never killed himself. The idea is absolutely ridiculous."

"Do you have any strong and valid reasons to suspect that someone would want to harm your son?"

Pam shook her head, just as furiously as she had nodded it moments before. "I thought about that all night. And it brought up some harsh truths about Kenny, sure. He had some guys that might not have cared too much for him because Kenny tended to steal women away from their boyfriends. But it never came to anything serious."

"And in the past few weeks, you hadn't heard Kenny say anything or act in a certain way that might indicate that he was having thoughts about hurting himself?"

"No. Nothing of the sort. Even when Kenny was in a bad mood, he managed to light up a room. He rarely even got angry about anything. He wasn't a perfect child but by God, I don't believe there was a single ounce of anger or hatred in him. I just find it absolutely beyond comprehension that he would have killed himself."

Another sob escaped her throat between the words *killed* and *himself.*

"Do you know if he had any sort of ties to that bridge?" Mackenzie asked.

"No more than the other teens and young adults in town. I'm sure he likely did some drinking or some flirting down there, but nothing out of the ordinary."

Mackenzie could sense the dam about to break within Pam Skinner. Another minute or two and she was going to snap.

"One more question, and please know that I have to ask it. But how certain are you that you knew your son well? Do you think there might have been some second life secrets he was keeping from you and your husband?"

She thought for a moment as tears trailed down her eyes. Slowly, she said, "I suppose anything is possible. But if Kenny *was* hiding some sort of second life from us, he was doing it with the skill of a spy. And while he was a great kid, he was not very committed to things. For him to have to hide something like that..."

"I follow you," Mackenzie said. "I'm going to leave you to deal with this now. But please, if you think of anything else in the coming days, call me right away."

With that, Mackenzie got to her feet and placed her business card on the countertop. "I'm so very sorry for your loss, Mrs. Skinner."

Mackenzie left quickly but not in a rude way. She could feel the weight of the family's loss until she was back outside, the door closed behind her. And even then, on the way to her car, she could hear the sounds of Pam Skinner finally letting out her grief. It was beyond haunting and it broke Mackenzie's heart a little bit.

Even when she was out of the driveway, the noise of Pam Skinner's crying swept through her head like a fall breeze rattling dead leaves across an abandoned street.

CHAPTER EIGHT

There was no coroner in the entire county. Even the Office of the Medical Examiner was an hour and a half away from Kingsville, located in Arlington. Rather than driving back to DC only to most likely head right back to Kingsville, Mackenzie returned to her motel room and made a series of calls. Ten minutes later, she was phoning into a Skype session with the coroner who had overseen the Malory Thomas's and Kenny Skinner's bodies. Kenny Skinner's body was not yet fully prepared and ready to evaluate, so that made things a bit harder.

Still, Mackenzie placed the call and waited for an answer. The man on the other end was one whom Mackenzie had worked with a few times on other cases, a middle-aged man with wiry gray hair named Barry Burke. It was nice to see a familiar face after the morning she'd had. She still couldn't quite shake the sounds of loss that had come out of Pam Skinner as she left their house.

"Hey there, Agent White," Burke said.

"Hey. So I'm being told that there's not much we can get from the body of Kenny Skinner yet, is that right?"

"I'm afraid so. At the risk of sounding crude, it's a pretty big mess. If you let me know what you're looking for, I can send it to the top of the priorities list."

"Any fresh scratches or bruising. Any signs that he might have been involved in a struggle."

"Will do. Now…I assume you need to know the same about Malory Thomas, right?"

"That's right. Do you have anything?"

"You know, we might. I hate to say it, but when we get a body that is pretty obviously a suicide, there are certain things that instantly drop to the bottom of our list of priorities. So yes…we found something on Malory Thomas that, in all honesty, could be nothing. But if you're looking for scratches…"

"What do you have?" she asked.

"Give me one second and I'll shoot you a picture," he said. He clicked around for a while and then the paperclip icon popped up in the Skype window.

Mackenzie clicked it and a JPEG opened up on her screen. She was looking at the underside of Malory Thomas's right hand.

Mackenzie zoomed in on the picture and saw what Burke was talking about right away. Between the first and second knuckle of three of the fingers, there were very apparent cuts and abrasions. The cuts looked very ragged and, while not bloody, raw and grisly all the same. There were two very large scratches on the upper part of her palm that looked like they might also be fairly recent. Lastly, there appeared to be some form of very faint indention in the meat of her hand just above the palm, making a small half-circle shape. For some reason, this one stuck out more so than the others. It seemed odd, and that usually meant it was the smoking gun she was looking for.

"Does that help you at all?" Burke asked.

"I don't know yet," Mackenzie said. "But it's more than what I had a minute ago."

"Also, this might be of note...one second." Burke rolled away from his desk for about ten seconds and then came back into view. He was holding a small plastic bag. Inside of it was what looked like a piece of tree bark. He held it closer to the camera. Mackenzie saw a piece of wood about an inch wide and an inch and a half long.

"This was in her hair," Burke said. "And the only reason we found it interesting is because it was the only piece of it in her hair. Usually when something like this is found on a body, particularly in the hair, there's a good amount of it. Wood chips, mulch, things like that. But this was the only piece."

"Weird question for you," Mackenzie said. "Can you snap a picture of that and send it to my email?"

"Hey, that's one of the *least* weird requests I've gotten this week. Job perks, you know..."

"Thanks for the meeting," Mackenzie said. "Any idea when you'll be able to get a better look at Kenny Skinner?"

"I'm hoping within a few hours."

"I hope to be back in DC tonight. I'll reach out when I get back and hopefully be able to make it by there."

With those plans set in place, they ended the call. Mackenzie emailed the picture of Malory Thomas's palm to her cell phone and then headed out at once. She thought of the scrapes and the barely there indention on the woman's hand, as well as the single piece of wood. It all meant something...she could feel it trying to click into place in her head.

Rather than puzzle it over in the motel, she figured there was no better place to go over it than the scene of the alleged crime. Her only hope was that Miller Moon Bridge was less somber and sinister-looking in the light of day.

***

When she reached the turn-off that led to the gravel road that dead-ended at Miller Moon Bridge, she was pleased to see a county police car parked along the edge. The bored-looking officer looked up when she pulled her car in alongside his. She flashed her badge and he waved her on after squinting closely at it.

Within a quarter of a mile, she reached the END STATE MAINTENANCE sign. It was at this point that the road became nothing but gravel. She took it slowly, listening to the crunch of pebbles beneath the car while it kicked up dust. After another mile or so, the first white struts of Miller Moon Bridge came into view, rising slightly in the air at a slanted angle. She came around a bend and then saw the whole thing, stretched out over the drop-off where a very dry riverbed sat underneath. While it didn't look quite as spooky in the daylight, the structure *did* show its age.

She parked several feet away from where the wooden planks began. She tried to imagine driving a car to the other side of this thing thirty or forty years ago and the mere thought of it terrified her. As she stepped onto the planks, she looked to the other side. There were two concrete barriers standing about four feet tall between the end of the bridge and the start of a road that was clearly no longer being used. It quite literally felt like she was stepping out onto the very edge of the world, where everything came to an end.

As she walked slowly along the bridge, she pulled up the picture of Malory's palm. She also opened the attachment in the email Burke had sent her after the Skype call. She opened up the image of the small piece of wood, having them both at the ready. She had no idea what she was looking for but felt confident she'd know it when her eyes fell on it.

As it turned out, that didn't take very long.

She'd made it about ten feet across the bridge when she noticed the layout of the beams and struts that ran along the sides of the bridge. They all, of course, ran underneath it for support, but on the other side of the white rails that separated the bridge from the open space beyond, there was a single iron strut that stuck out about two feet wider than the bridge. It was just wide enough for someone to step out onto.

She looked down the length of the bridge and counted three different struts. She went to the rail and hunkered down to get a

35

closer look. The strut in front of her also supported five smaller struts than ran beneath the bridge. These smaller ones were attached to the larger ones with large bolts. The bolts were capped off with what looked like smooth metal caps, worn and rusted with age.

Mackenzie looked at the picture of Malory's palm, zooming in on the indentation in her skin. Slightly circular, the curves looking very much like the circumference of the metal caps on the strut.

She ran her finger carefully over the metal cap. Yes, it was smooth—probably put there to hide the rougher edging of whatever industrial bolt had been used to attach the struts—but the edges of the caps were a little rough around the edges.

Mackenzie got back to her feet and slowly walked a bit farther down the bridge. She saw the same layout, one after another. Five bolts, the ends of which were covered by those smooth iron caps. There would then be a break in the spacing of the caps, and then there would be five more. She counted three sets of five in the first iron strut, and then five in the next.

She didn't get to the third iron strut on the last portion of the bridge, though. When she was about halfway down the bridge, she came to a spot where the wooden base of the bridge's frame poked out just a bit from beyond the iron strut. Not much…maybe three inches. But it was enough for Mackenzie to realize that the beams and struts beneath the bridge were partially made of wood—perhaps just the original frame or additional construction.

She again went to her knees and leaned a bit out past the safety railings. She ran her hand along the little bit of exposed wood. It was old and brittle but quite hard. She compared the color and texture of the wood to the small piece that Burke had bagged and showed to her. Even with the glare of her cell phone, she could tell that it was the same.

But if she jumped, how the hell did it get into her hair?

She was pretty sure the picture of Malory's palm answered that question.

If the indention of one of those caps was on her palm, she didn't jump. She was hanging *from the bridge…maybe trying to save herself. And the wood chip in her hair…if she was hanging from this very spot, it's not too hard to believe that this old wood might have flaked off into her hair as she tried to regain her grip.*

She ran her thumb over the five caps along the strut in front of her one by one. At the one second to the end, she felt a roughness to the cap's ending. It was certainly rough enough to cause those paper-thin abrasions on Malory's hand.

With her heart in her chest, Mackenzie looked down over the rail. The rocks that had ultimately killed Malory Thomas and Kenny Skinner waited down there. Even from this height, she could see the discoloration where there had been blood less than twelve hours ago.

I'm standing where they stood, Mackenzie thought. *They were standing right here moments before they died.*

She then looked back to the picture of the indentation in Malory's palm, and then back to the bolt caps. And then she corrected her thought: *They were standing right here moments before they were* murdered.

CHAPTER NINE

Mackenzie did not have cell phone reception until she was back off of the gravel road so she wasn't able to call McGrath with an update for another ten minutes. His secretary said he was out of the office and he did not answer his cell phone. She decided not to leave a message and, instead, called up Sheriff Tate.

Tate didn't answer either but as his voicemail kicked on, she remembered him telling her how his outdated phone had been misbehaving. She hung up, frustrated, but before she had time to get angry, Tate called her directly back.

"Told ya," he said. "This damned phone. Anyway, what can I do for you, Agent White?" he asked.

"How quickly can you meet me at the station with a few of your best men?"

"I'm at the station right now. And if it's concerning Kenny Skinner, then the only other person that knows is my deputy, like I told you last night. I can have him back here in about twenty minutes. Why? What's up?"

"Just some things I want to fill you in on."

"You find something?" he asked, instantly curious. He also sounded a bit excited and Mackenzie wasn't sure how to take that.

"I'd really rather wait until I can meet you there. By the way…do you have any way for me to dial in to DC?"

"Just a standard old touchtone phone. We can conference someone in if we need to."

She felt a little spoiled when she found this disappointing. Regardless, she thanked him and ended the call.

She was five minutes away from the Kingsville PD when McGrath called her back. After she went over the details of what she had found, he went silent for a moment. Finally, just as she was about to pull into the station's lot, he spoke.

"You're certain of this?" he asked.

"I'm certain enough to say that it strongly warrants an investigation."

"That's good enough for me. Find some way to bring me into this meeting you're about to have. I want to stay close on this one."

"Will do. Give me a few minutes."

She parked and went into the station. Sheriff Tate was sitting behind the little bullpen area, waiting for her. When she came into the lobby, he walked quickly to meet her right away. As he escorted her to the back of the small building, he spoke to her under his breath.

"I did manage to get one of my guys to figure out a way to hook you up with a video call sort of thing on one of our laptops. I'm sure it's not as high tech as what you're used to in DC, but it's all we got out here."

"It's okay. That should be fine."

Tate led her into a conference room where a rather old MacBook was sitting on a small wooden table. Another man sat at the end of the table, giving her a wave as she came in. He then stood up and offered his hand.

"Deputy Andrews," he said. "Nice to meet you, Agent White." He was a short and stout man, a little on the heavy side, with the sort of gritty southern charm that could be either charming or off-putting. Mackenzie couldn't decide where Andrews fell just yet.

"So, this is the best we could do," Tate said, turning the MacBook in her direction. "My guy just made sure FaceTime was operable on it. That's high-tech shit for Kingsville."

She pulled McGrath's number from her contact list and typed it in. When she placed the call, it took a few moments before it connected. When McGrath's face came on the screen, Tate and Andrews crowded in behind Mackenzie.

A quick round of introductions were made—nothing more than a formality really, as she was sure McGrath couldn't care less about Kingsville's finest.

"For the sake of all being on the same page," Mackenzie said, "I'm going to go over everything one more time. There were very minor abrasions on Malory Thomas's left palm. There was also a very faint indention of sorts, as if she had been clutching on to something moments before her death. After visiting the Miller Moon Bridge this morning, I was able to determine that the indentation was the exact shape of the end caps placed on the bolts along the struts on the edge of the bridge.

"Additionally, there was a piece of wood found in her hair—which the coroner found off because it was the *only* piece. It just so happens that the scrap of wood in her hair is the exact same as the wooden planks along and underneath the bridge, right down to the tone and texture. Put all of this together with the fact that she was nude and her clothes were discovered on the bridge, it makes me think she did not jump. It seems more like she was dangling on the edge of the bridge. Pretty tightly, I might add, based on that indentation. And if she was going to kill herself, why would she struggle to hold on to the edge?"

"Makes sense to me," Tate said.

"Yes, it does," McGrath said. "But that then leads us to more questions. Was it just Malory Thomas who might have been murdered? Can we also lump Kenny Skinner in with her? And if so, why not everyone else who has jumped from that bridge?"

"I spoke with Dr. Jan Haggerty, a psychiatrist here in town. She says that based on what she knew of Kenny Skinner, there was no way he committed suicide. His mother strongly agrees. And if you look at the dates of the suicides, it's been almost two years since a body was found on the rocks beneath the bridge. Now, two years later, we have two within the span of four days. I think it's a safe assumption to say that Kenny Skinner's death might be worth looking into as a murder as well. The timing makes it too concrete to be a coincidence."

"Sheriff Tate, we've discussed the importance of the Skinner kid already," McGrath said. "I ask that in the coming days you please consider giving Agent White any assistance she needs. And please let her have full run of this case. She's among my best agents and I trust her completely. Can you do that for me?"

"Absolutely. Just let us know how we can help."

"Agent White, do you have any leads to pursue at this point?"

"Nothing solid," she said. "But I imagine it wouldn't be too hard to find some people to speak with in regards to the lives of the victims. I'm continuously being told how this is one of those towns where everybody knows everybody. Speaking to Kenny Skinner's mother gave me a few ideas."

"Good. Get to it, and keep me posted. Sheriff Tate, thanks again for your cooperation."

"No pro—"

But McGrath had hung up, the screen glitching for a moment and then the call coming to an end.

"Don't take it personally," Mackenzie said. "He does that to me all the time."

With a shrug, Tate asked, "So what do you need from us?"

Mackenzie thought for a moment, trying to determine the best course of action. "Can you get me the police records for any of the people who have committed suicide from the bridge in the last five years or so?"

"I can get that for you," Miller said. "But I don't think there will be too much to look at."

"That's fine, just—"

Her phone rang, interrupting her. She answered it and heard Pam Skinner's somber voice on the other end.

"Agent White? Are you still in Kingsville?"

"I am."

"Do you think you could come back over to our house? My husband has finally sort of calmed down and would like to speak with you."

"Of course. Just give me a few minutes."

It wasn't a lead, per se, but it was better than what she had at the moment. And just like that, Mackenzie left the Kingsville PD more certain than ever that she was officially looking for a murderer.

CHAPTER TEN

When Mackenzie pulled into the Skinners' driveway ten minutes later, she saw a man that she assumed to be Vincent Skinner on the front porch. He was sitting rigidly in an old rocker, his eyes trailing her car as she pulled in. When she joined him on the porch, she could see quite clearly that he was wrecked. His eyes were red from crying and his entire body seemed like one tightly coiled knot, ready to snap at the next sign of pressure.

"Mr. Skinner, thanks for taking the time to speak with me."

"Thank *you* for looking into this," he said. "I figured we'd meet out here. Pam is finally letting herself sleep so I want to keep the house nice and quiet."

"That's understandable."

"Pam told me all the things she told you and I have to agree with her one hundred percent," Vincent said. "Kenny just wasn't the sort of young man that would kill himself. As cheesy as it sounds, he loved life too much."

"Can you give me some examples?"

Vincent looked to the porch boards at his feet and chuckled, a sad sound coming out of his hoarse throat. "Well, I won't paint a pretty picture for you. I mean, I loved my son without fail but he could be a little troublesome at times. He had this crappy apartment on the outskirts of town and he'd been working for me for years, so I *know* the kind of money he was making. He also dabbled in some stupid stock market apps, bringing in a little money here and there like that. But still...a new girl seemingly every month, partying on the weekends but never to excess...but despite all that, he was well-mannered. And I feel confident that anyone else in town would tell you the same. He was polite, kind-hearted...but he liked to have his fun, too."

"These woman he saw," Mackenzie said. "Is there any chance there might be a jealous ex-boyfriend that could have been seeking revenge?"

"If so, I wouldn't know about it. I do know, though, that the last two girls he was fooling around with were single at the time."

"And do you know their names?"

"Lizzy was one...but I don't remember her last name. She wasn't from Kingsville. She was from Elm Creek, two towns over. The one before her was Amanda Armstrong. She lives here in town. Had a divorce a few years back. I sort of poked fun at him because she was damn near twelve years older than he was. But her ex moved away to Boston, I think. So I don't think there'd be any chance of him being involved."

"Well, what about at work? He worked for you and you run a tractor supply store, is that correct?"

"Yeah, tire and tractor. Kenny was good at what he did but really didn't put a lot of passion into it."

"And what was he responsible for at work?"

"I had him and one other guy in charge of all tire sales," Vincent answered. "Kenny was also pretty good with small repairs to cars, trucks, and farm equipment."

"And did he get along with his co-workers?"

"Yeah. They're the ones he'd usually party with on the weekends. They could be irresponsible at times but I never had any problems with them. Well...I take that back. There was one time, about eight or nine months ago I guess, where Kenny just about got into a fist fight with a guy in the parking lot."

"A customer?"

"Well, a would-be customer. He came to the shop for a few tractor tires from what I understand. But he and Kenny had some words and it got really heated. I wasn't there that day; one of the other guys had to break it up."

"And you don't know what the argument was about?"

"No. And Kenny never told me."

"Do you recall the name of the man?"

"Oh yeah. It was J.T. Case. He's a local guy. Has a pretty sizable cornfield about ten miles from here."

"And is he known to be a troublemaker?"

"No, not J.T. But his son, Mike, is a little asshole. One of those guys that was always bullying kids in school. I hate to spread gossip but there's a rumor that he beat one of his ex-girlfriends half to death. He was gone for about a year and then came back. No one is really sure what happened, to be honest."

"But the argument at work was between J.T.—the father—and Kenny, right?"

"That's right."

Mackenzie took all of this in, not feeling that there was much to go on but wanting *something* to start building some leads.

"Lastly, is there *anyone* you can think of who might have something against your son—something so bad that they'd be driven to murder?"

"I've been thinking about that ever since we learned that he had died. The moment Sheriff Tate told me that it looked like suicide, I knew it was bullshit. I instantly started wondering who would want to kill Kenny and I couldn't come up with a single person."

Mackenzie nodded and got to her feet. "Well, you have my card if you *do* think of anything else. Don't hesitate to call me even if you think of something that might seem trivial."

"Sure," Vincent said, but he already had a faraway look in his eyes. He was looking to the porch boards at his feet again, perhaps trying to figure out how this had all happened—how his life had literally changed overnight.

Mackenzie returned to her car and backed out of the driveway, feeling like she'd accomplished nothing through this meeting other than causing a grieving man to dig even deeper into his pain.

***

When she arrived back at the station, there seemed to be more energy about the place. She assumed this was because the two recent suicides were now officially being investigated as murder cases. When she returned to the small conference room, she found Deputy Andrews and another officer poring over several stacks of files.

"Get anything from the father?" Andrews asked.

"I don't know yet," Mackenzie said. "There's still just too much digging to do. I may need to head back out to the bridge to get a better look at the rocks down below in the daylight. Maybe there's something there that was missed."

"Maybe," Andrews said, though this tone indicated that he wasn't really so sure about it.

"Well, I think I might have *something* for you," said the other officer. He was a younger-looking African-American guy, maybe in his late twenties. The tag above his left breast read Roberts. He slid two files over to her with a hopeful look in his eye.

"What am I looking at?" Mackenzie asked.

"The files for Malory Thomas and Carl Alvarez."

"Alvarez," Mackenzie said. It took her a moment to recover the name from her memory. He had been on the list of suicides from Miller Moon Bridge over the course of the last several years.

44

"Yes," Roberts said. "He jumped off the bridge four years ago. At first glance, there's really not much that ties the two of them together. Only Alvarez has a record and the only charge against him was possession of marijuana from the very same year he killed himself. However, it's *how* he got the marijuana that connects them. It seems the guy that sold Alvarez the pot also has a connection to Malory Thomas. Got into a fight with her ex-boyfriend not too long ago."

"Seems like a pretty solid connection," Mackenzie said. "Who's the guy?"

And even before she got her answer, she was pretty much expecting it. Sometimes, a case just fell together that way.

Roberts answered: "Mike Case."

CHAPTER ELEVEN

Mackenzie was quickly coming to understand that when teens didn't leave small towns after high school, they often ended up working for their parents somehow or another. It had been true for Kenny Skinner and it was apparently true of Mike Case as well. Sheriff Tate had placed a call to J.T. Case and had gotten confirmation that Mike Case was working on the crops today, out at the Cases' farm.

Because J.T. Case was known to be something of a hard ass—although a well-respected hard ass—Tate had insisted on accompanying her. She had tried to convince him that she'd be fine, but he wasn't having it. Because it wasn't worth the argument, Mackenzie relented.

Mackenzie could have found the farm easy enough even without Tate behind the wheel of his cruiser. The cornfield stuck out immediately on the right side of the highway just as she had driven out of the Kingsville town limits. Seeing the corn sent her mind spiraling back to Nebraska, where her journey had started. She recalled walking through the tall stalks when the Scarecrow Killer case had been ramping up—seeing the bodies tied to the posts as if beckoning her forward into a future she wasn't sure about.

When Tate parked the car, Mackenzie took note of the two men attaching a small platform trailer to the back of an older-model GMC pickup. They both looked up the patrol car, seemed to not really even notice them, and then went back to attaching the trailer.

Mackenzie and Tate walked up to the pickup truck. She figured she'd let Tate kick things off since he seemed to have a read on J.T. Case. She was more interested in getting a read on Mike, though. She wondered if this was going to be the kind of tight-knit southern family that stuck together no matter what. Would the father still protect his twenty-something boy as if he were a helpless toddler?

"Hey there, J.T.," Tate said. "You too, Mike. How's things going?"

"Not too bad," J.T. said. He slipped a bolt through the hatch of the trailer, connecting it to the truck. "I'm about to take this trailer out there and round up the dead stalks, so if we can make this quick, I'd appreciate it."

"Well, I'm just here as a friendly escort, really. I want you to meet Agent White, from the FBI. She's here to look into the recent deaths."

Both of the Cases looked up at Mackenzie with great interest. Apparently, the mention of the FBI had broken them out of their stubborn *I-don't-care* attitudes.

"Deaths?" J.T. asked. "Don't you mean *suicides*?"

"Well, that's what they both look like from a distance," Mackenzie said. "But further investigations have led us to believe that there was foul play involved in at least one of them."

"That don't mean it's the case for all of them, now does it?" Mike said.

"Well, that's what I'm trying to find out. The tricky thing is that there are so many of these suicides from that bridge over the years that it's hard to individualize each one. So what we did was look for links between them and so far, there's only one link to be found."

"Tell me, Mike," Tate said. "You remember getting in a fight last year with a guy named Chris Osborne?"

Mike scoffed a bit and nodded his head. "Yeah. What about him?"

"You happen to know who he was dating at the time?"

This time, Mike outright laughed. "You've got to be kidding me. Yeah…he was with Malory Thomas at the time."

"And what was the fight about?" Mackenzie asked.

"Me and some friends were out at a bar. And maybe I said a few inappropriate things to Malory. Offered to buy her a few drinks. Chris didn't like it and ran his mouth. We ended up fighting. End of story."

"Sheriff, I don't appreciate what you two are suggesting," J.T. said.

"Hey, I don't either," Tate said. "But in regards to a case like this where there are very few leads, we have to go down every possible avenue. And right now, the only link we have between two of the victims is Mike."

"What other link?" Mike asked. "What other victim?"

"Carl Alvarez, from three years ago," Mackenzie said. "Records indicate that he was busted for possessing a pretty good stash of pot. He offered up your name, said you sold it to him."

He looked away quickly and as far as Mackenzie was concerned, that was proof of guilt. Still, he shook his head. "Yeah, I

47

got grilled hard for that," Mike said. He then looked directly at Tate and added: "But it never stuck, did it? Apparently chasing after people without any hard proof is what goes for police work in Kingsville."

Sensing some sort of local tension brewing, Mackenzie took charge of the conversation, steering back toward the matter at hand.

"Mike, if I asked you to provide proof of your whereabouts the last several nights, would you be able to do it?"

He went quiet for a moment. Mackenzie couldn't tell if he was trying to think of his alibis or deciding whether or not to allow the interrogation to continue. Finally, he crossed his arms and answered.

"Yes. For the last three nights, I've been out at Road Runner's bar, just down the road. Before that, I slept here for the night, crashing on the couch."

"You do that often?" Mackenzie asked.

"He does," J.T. said. "But I don't see how that's any of your business."

"So you can attest to the fact that Mike slept on your couch four nights ago?" Mackenzie asked.

"Yes. He gets these back spasms from time to time. The little idiot took four painkillers for it that afternoon and I wouldn't let him drive."

"And how about the bar?" Mackenzie asked Mike. "How did you pay?"

"Cash. But you can ask anyone that was there and they'll tell you. I was there until at least eleven at night. And then I went straight home....except last night when I caught a ride with a woman I've been seeing."

"Can we have her name and number?" Tate asked.

J.T. stepped in front of Mike and shook his head. "No. No, you can't. And I'm sorry, but I'm going to ask you to leave as nicely as I can. I am well aware that my son has made some poor choices, but to suggest that he killed anyone, much less pushed them from a bridge or some such shit, is insulting. He's given you more than enough information to prove his innocence and I will be damned if I'll continue to let you keep grilling him."

Tate seemed to get a little defensive over this, but Mackenzie was satisfied. She took a step back toward the car, nodding for Tate to follow her. "That's fine," she said. "Thank you for your time, gentlemen."

Tate followed her slowly back to the car, clearly a little confused. When he was back behind the wheel and starting the engine, he gave the Cases one last glance.

"That was all you needed?" he asked.

"Yes. A small town like this, it will be easy enough to figure out if Mike Case was indeed at the bar these last three nights. And if he was, it pretty much eliminates him from Kenny Skinner's death. And if his father is vouching for him having slept on the couch on the night Malory Thomas was killed, that clears him of that, too. I *would* like to have you send someone to the bar to make sure the story checks out. If it doesn't, we'll pay him a visit again…and this time with evidence that he's lying about something."

"What does your gut tell you?" Tate asked.

"I'm ninety-nine percent sure it's not Mike Case. Both he and his father were more concerned about us relentlessly asking questions and questioning his character than what he was being accused of. There's guilt and then there's defensiveness. Rarely will you see them so blended. Those guys were caught off guard by it all. They were legitimately baffled that we were trying to accuse Mike of murder."

Tate grinned. "Man…if your mind works like that all the time, you must stay exhausted."

She supposed it was a compliment. He was mostly wrong, though. It was when her thoughts fired on all cylinders that she felt the most energetic. It was, in fact, how she was feeling as they headed back to the station. She was on the trail of a killer who was likely a resident of the small town she was currently investigating. That usually meant that the conclusion to the case wasn't too far away.

But she also knew that those isolated cases could sometimes be more dangerous. She gave the cornfield one last wary look as they passed by, as if to remind herself of this.

CHAPTER TWELVE

Because the case was currently in a state of file-checking and waiting on coroner results, Mackenzie decided to head back to DC. There, she'd stop to visit Barry Burke at the medical examiner's office to see if things were any clearer in regards to the body of Kenny Skinner. The trip was only seventy minutes or so; if anything happened to come up in Kingsville while she was gone, she could be back there within an hour.

She headed out of Kingsville with all of this in mind. In the back of her head, she was also aware that she wanted to go back in order to check in with Ellington. Speaking to him on the phone was one thing, but having been lovers for several months and work partners even longer than that, there was much more she could gather from a face-to-face talk.

The transition from the backwoods of Kingsville to the interwoven roads and streets of DC and its suburbs was gradual but still managed to creep up on her. Before she was fully aware of how much time had passed, she found herself taking an exit toward an appointment she had set up over the phone with Barry Burke at the medical examiner's office.

It was 1:37 in the afternoon when she met with Burke in one of the examination rooms. The room had recently been cleaned and sterilized. The surfaces were shiny, the air thick with the smell of ammonia.

"I've got good news and bad news for you," Burke told her, leaning against one of the exam tables.

"Bad news first," she said.

"I found absolutely nothing on Kenny Skinner that would indicate there was any foul play involved. There was some bruising on his chest but quite frankly, there would be no way at all to determine if they were preexisting or not."

"So all of his injuries aligned with what you'd expect after someone dropped one hundred and seventy-five feet onto those rocks?"

"Yes, pretty much. In Kenny's case, I just hope the blow to the head killed him before the absolute devastation of his shattered back had time to register through his nerves. His spine was

50

shattered in a few places and two of his ribs had burst out of his skin."

"Yeah, that's bad news all right," Mackenzie said. "What's the good news?"

"Well, the good news is that because there was no evidence to support murder, I don't have to show you any of the grisly pictures."

"That *is* good news. I already saw it up close last night and that was in poor lighting. So yeah…I'm good not seeing it again. I do have a question for you, though. Can you look back through your records to see if the body of a guy named Carl Alvarez came through here sometime three years ago?"

"Yeah, I can check on that for you. You need it now or can I send it to you?"

"Just let me know as soon as you find out."

"Are you looking for the same kind of thing?" Burke asked. "Evidence of something that might point towards murder rather than suicide?"

"Yes, exactly."

"I can check but I have to tell you—suicides like these, jumpers from such a height—it's going to be very hard. Especially on bodies that have already come and gone."

"I expected as much," she said. "But I'd still like to know for sure."

Burke nodded at her. And even though he said nothing, the look on his face told her that he understood her desperation. Other than the revelation about Malory Thomas hanging from the edge of the bridge, she really didn't have much to go on. She was, essentially, chasing ghosts.

***

Her next stop was the J. Edgar Hoover Building. It had been her place of employment for more than a year now but she still found it hard to believe that the often bashful woman who had started out as a plainclothes cop in Nebraska had ended up here. She walked up to her office, feeling as if she was returning empty-handed. True, it had been her work and insight that had pushed the so-called suicide cases to a murder investigation, but then what? If anything, she had really done nothing more than escalate a situation that seemed to lead them straight to a dead end.

She ventured up to McGrath's office and he was able to see her right away. He looked stressed when she sat down in front of his desk. She was starting to wonder just how much pressure the deputy director was placing on him to get to the bottom of his nephew's death.

"Strangely enough," McGrath said, "Director Wilmoth is more relieved to know that there's a chance his nephew was killed. I suppose murder is a more sympathetic cause of death than suicide. He describes his extended family as being very much about appearances. If it were a suicide, of course, his name might be brought up in the news. By the way, good job of keeping this a secret. In a small town like Kingsville, it can't be easy."

"I get the impression that the PD down there wants it just as quiet as we do. They don't exactly enjoy the fact that they have a landmark that people are using as a literal suicide machine."

"Any new developments?" McGrath asked.

"I spoke with one potential lead this morning. Kingsville PD is following up on alibis but I am fairly certain it's going to end up in a dead end. I also stopped by the medical examiner's office on the way here. They weren't able to find any evidence of murder on the body of Kenny Skinner."

"Yeah, I just spoke to the head ME down there. We've got some forensics guys headed down there right now, but no one is really thinking we'll find anything. So what are the next steps?"

"I don't know that there *are* any," Mackenzie said. "Kingsville PD has the road to the bridge under surveillance. They're checking the one possible suspect's alibis. There was no evidence at the scene…so I don't know. Aside from meeting with every single friend and every single family member of every single suicide victim over the last few years, I don't see any real solution."

"At the risk of sounding like an ass, I think maybe that's just what you need to do. Go back down there and stay. Talk to anyone you think might have even the *slightest* bit of information. We want this done as fast as possible, so you have my permission to stay down there as long as you have to."

"Yes sir."

"Did you come back because of Ellington?" he asked.

She saw no need in lying. "Partly," she said. "But I needed to get by to speak with Burke as well. And while I'm here, I'll go ahead and update my notes. But I'll make a point to get back down there no later than five this afternoon."

"Sounds good," he said. "Stay on top of this one, White. If you can find an actual killer, Wilmoth is going to take notice. And that could do amazing things for your career."

She nodded and left the office, feeling the added pressure of knowing that people higher up the bureau ladder were paying close attention to her on this one. It remained on her mind as she typed up her notes in her office. She felt like she was being scrutinized, studied closer than she had ever been before.

And while it was nerve-wracking, it also motivated her. Already, her thoughts were turning back to that old bridge—the bolts, the struts, the stomach-churning drop to the rocks below.

But first, there was Ellington.

And if the conversation didn't go right, she figured that might be just as bad as staring down off of that bridge and to the ground below.

***

He wasn't in the apartment when she got there, so she called his cell. He told her that he was in the park five blocks from their house, getting in a run. She opted to walk instead of drive, figuring she still had plenty of time if she had until five to return to Kingsville. She found him standing at a bench, doing some post-run stretches. He smiled widely when he saw her and then dropped it when she did not return it.

"How long of a run?" she asked.

"Three and a half miles."

"Taking it light today, I see."

"Just lazy. After everything that has happened, I can't seem to find the motivation. And when you can't find the focus to do something as simple as run…"

"So then let's talk about it. I need to get back to Kingsville pretty soon."

"Going back? What's the deal down there anyway?"

She frowned. She hated keeping secrets from him but she knew that she was being watched closely. "Sorry," she said. "McGrath wants me to keep it quiet."

"Would you still be keeping it quiet if things hadn't progressed the way they had over the last day and a half or so? About the allegations against me?"

"Well, if you hadn't been asked to leave, you might be on the case with me," she said a little bitterly. "So that's a moot question."

"Fair enough," he said.

With that, they both took a seat on the bench and looked out to the park.

"I'll admit that I have no idea why this bothers me so badly," Mackenzie said. "I think it comes down to a sense of trust. It's something I feel you should have told me, especially before we moved in together."

"Probably," he admitted. "But I was ashamed, you know? And honestly, at the time it seemed really insignificant. And that's where I'm struggling right now. Because at the time, it *did* seem insignificant. I don't know why it's all of a sudden a big deal."

"How did the conversation with McGrath go?" she asked. "Is the woman looking for anything?"

"Other than to make me look bad and make me uncomfortable? I don't know."

Mackenzie nearly asked for the woman's name. Maybe she'd pull her name from the database and see what kind of a woman she was. It was hard for her to imagine a woman holding a grudge for so long and then seeking her revenge when the political climate was perfect for her claim.

"You want me to move out?" Ellington asked.

"No. I just…I don't know. I have to work at letting people get close. I don't naturally let people in. This just sort of blindsided me. And besides…you're a good partner."

"At work or in bed?" he asked with a sly smile.

"Don't push it."

They fell quiet after that. When he reached out and took her hand, she let him. "I'll get over it," she said. "I didn't know you then. If anything, I think I'm more worried about your character…doing that sort of thing while you were married."

"I know. But I learned my lesson. That's why I had to turn down a very attractive detective in Nebraska not too long ago. And that was *hard*."

She smiled in spite of herself. She gave his hand a squeeze and then got to her feet. "I need to get back. I'll call you later tonight. You good?"

"Yeah. Just curious about this secret case you're on."

Mackenzie made a zipping gesture across her lips and shot him a smile. "Keep being curious, then. I like being a mysterious woman."

She left it at that, walking back the way she had come. Part of her badly wanted to talk to him about the case. Maybe he could identify with her. There was one thing about the case that was making her hesitant, something that kept her from really diving in and committing. It was not something she would dare tell McGrath. But she could tell Ellington in any other circumstance.

She could tell Ellington that she was afraid of heights.

She could tell him that looking down from Miller Moon Bridge had scared the hell out of her. She could tell him how she'd almost fallen out of a pine tree when she was eight years old, how she'd dangled thirty or so feet in the air, the sap clinging to her fingers while her little heart hammered in her chest.

But of course, with this case, she couldn't tell him any of that.

She half-expected him to walk her back to her car but he didn't. She actually appreciated this. It showed her that he knew her strange little quirks and respected them. He knew when she needed distance and he respected it.

On her way to the car, she pulled out her phone and called up Tate. He answered with hope in his voice, maybe assuming she'd managed to crack the case in DC.

"Any luck?" he asked.

"No. But I'm heading back. Do me a favor, would you. Can you or one of your officers put together a list of close family and friends for Malory Thomas? Skip the parents. I think friends would be best for now."

"Just as well," Tate said. "Her father is in prison somewhere in North Carolina and her mom passed away when she was a teenager. She's got an aunt in town. And yeah, I can rustle up the names of a few friends."

"Thanks. See you soon."

"Agent White...tell me. Shoot straight with me. You think we've got a killer in our town?"

"I just don't know yet," she said.

It felt and sounded weak coming out of her mouth. And she really hoped that Sheriff Tate wasn't adept at picking out a lie when he heard one.

CHAPTER THIRTEEN

Maureen Hanks looked out the windshield and saw the looming shape of the Kingsville water tower. In the thick darkness of night, it stood out like a giant ghoul, always haunting the town. And because the town was so small, it sometimes served as a lighthouse of sorts, there to help people find the center of town.

Of course, Maureen was not in the center of town. She was in the front seat of Bob Tully's pickup, parked at the edge of an old overgrown hayfield. She was putting her bra back on, her fingers still trembling from the intensity her body had just experienced. She was out of breath, as was Bob, both wiped out from the physical exertions of the last ten minutes. The truck smelled like sweat, sex, and faintly of the sweet cheap wine she always drank when she met up with Bob.

She looked away from the shape of the water tower and over to Bob as he bent awkwardly back into the seat to pull his pants up. She took a moment to admire his defined abs and the hard yet small muscles of his arms, all the result of lifting and welding at his job at Connor Trucking. Seeing his body in the moments after sex, when their sweat was on one another and her nerves were still jumpy, made her recall how she had so easily fallen into this affair. It made it much easier to push down the guilt that reared its head when she thought of her husband and her three year-old daughter back at home.

"Don't take this the wrong way," Bob said. "But we can't do this again."

"You say that every time," she said, reaching over and running her hand over his stomach. "And about two days later, we end up here."

"I know," he said. "But it's got to stop. You understand that, right? This fucking town is too small. People will find out. And I'm not going to be the guy that causes a family to split up."

They'd been in the midst of this affair for six months now. She wondered why he all of a sudden concerned himself with the state of her marriage.

"Fine," she said. She knew he'd change his mind. He'd get horny again in a few days and leave her a little note under the bench behind Homeland Realty, where she worked. She'd have him again…and again and again.

And if not…well then maybe she'd finally figure out how to find happiness in the domesticated life she thought she'd wanted four years ago when she had married her husband.

Bob gave her one final look as she slid her shirt on. She liked the way he looked at her—it was one of the reasons the affair had started in the first place. Her husband had stopped looking at her like that after they'd had their daughter.

Bob cranked the engine to life and backed out of their private spot. The truck bumped across the field until they found the small dirt road that etched itself back to the back roads of Kingsville. It was there, just out of sight of the road, that she had parked her car. They said nothing to one another as he stopped the truck. She leaned over to him and they exchanged a kiss, an intense and borderline sloppy kiss that could not strike a balance between passion and lust.

"See you around," she said as she opened the door and stepped out. She walked to her car and got behind the wheel. She sat there for a while, watching Bob's truck disappear around the curb in the dirt road. She closed her eyes for a moment, listening to the quiet of the country night.

This is nuts, she thought. *I have a beautiful family, a husband that might still love me if I gave him a chance, and a gorgeous daughter.*

She opened her eyes and reached for her keys. For a moment, something felt strange. Something felt…*off.*

It was probably just her nerves. She was always paranoid after meeting with Bob, feeling as if there were eyes in the forest, spying on her.

She cranked the car and shifted it into drive. But before her foot touched the pedal, a voice rose up out of the back seat as something hard and cold was placed at the base of her skull.

***

He'd known Maureen Hanks and Bob Tully had been having an affair for about a month. He'd been scouting out secret places in Kingsville, places that rose up high above the ground. The water tower had come to mind and that's where he'd seen them first. Bob's truck had been squeaking lightly. He'd hidden behind a copse of trees about twenty feet away and watched, seeing Maureen topless through the windshield and hearing her squeals and moans of pleasure.

He'd never liked Maureen. Her parents were assholes; they thought they owned the town. And she'd been a massive bitch in high school. He had noticed this even though she'd been three years ahead of him, graduating when he had only finished ninth grade.

And now here she was, sitting in front of him, with his gun placed to the back of her head. He could smell the sex on her. He wondered how her husband never noticed it. Or maybe he did and just didn't care. He assumed Maureen Hanks was not the sort of woman worth fighting for.

"What have you been up to?" he asked her.

He saw her trying to look in her rearview. He pressed the barrel harder to the back of her head. She had no way of knowing it wasn't loaded. Tricking her like this made him feel even more in control.

"I asked you a question," he said. "What have you been up to? Just now...what were you doing?"

"Please...please don't tell anyone."

"Oh, I don't care about your affair. I just want to hear you say it."

"I was having sex."

"With your husband?"

"No."

"With Bob Tully," he said. "A man I'm sure is just as equally terrible as you."

She let out a sob here and he noticed her shaking. "Please...I'll do anything. Just please don't tell anyone. And don't...please don't use that gun."

"I'm sure you *would* do anything," he said. "Fucking Bob Tully is proof of that. And don't worry...I won't use the gun unless you make me. For now, I just need you to do exactly what I tell you."

"Yes, okay. What?"

"The water tower...you know how to get to the access road?"

She hesitated here and lightly shook her head. She was as stiff as a board in the seat in front of him. "No, I don't think so."

"It's easy," he said. "We're going to take a trip to it. I'll give you directions. For right now, you just drive."

"Why the water tower?" she asked.

He smiled in the darkness of her back seat, the place he had been waiting for her while she had been with Bob. He'd been hiding out, knowing they'd be there. He'd followed Bob around Kingsville when he got off work. He watched Bob place the note under that bench. He'd then later followed the truck out here, parking his car

58

about a mile away and then hiking through the woods and reaching her car moments after Maureen had gotten into Bob's truck.

"Just go. Get back to the road and take a left."

"Okay," she said, weeping now. "But why?"

Swallowing down a chuckle, he answered: "For the view."

CHAPTER FOURTEEN

Mackenzie pulled her car into the parking lot of Road Runner's, the same little bar that Mike Case apparently frequented. Deputy Andrews and Officer Roberts had worked quickly to get a contact list together for those who knew Malory Thomas the best. In the end, the only names on the list that really resulted in anything were Emma Huddleston and Michelle Nash. When Mackenzie had called them on her way back into Kingsville, they'd made arrangements to meet at Road Runner's since that's where Emma and Michelle had already planned on meeting later that night anyway.

The place was the very definition of a dive bar. It was located next to what appeared to be a long forgotten Blockbuster Video, the logo still somewhat readable in the dust where the sticker had once stood in the window. There were neon signs in the bar's windows, flashing advertisements for different brands of beer; the Road Runner's logo, however, was done in simple vinyl on the double doors that served as its entrance.

Before Mackenzie walked inside, she passed by a group of people smoking just outside the door. Apparently smoking had been banned from bars even in the most remote of areas. Looking around inside, she felt more than a little judgmental. The place didn't really do much to make it seem as if it was trying to class itself up. An ancient jukebox sat against the far wall, where three men huddled around it, one playing air guitar to "Money for Nothing" by the Dire Straits.

The actual bar was a simple stretch of wood that ran along half of the left wall. There were only three beer taps behind the bar, with several shelves of liquor behind an overweight bartender who was currently mixing soda into what looked like rum.

She found Emma and Michelle exactly where they'd said they'd be. They were both blonde, both fairly skinny, and very young-looking. Yet as she got closer, she saw that the one on the left was at least thirty, trying to knock about ten years from her appearance with the help of makeup. They were sitting in a corner booth with a pitcher of beer and three glasses centered on the table, two of which were partially filled.

"Emma and Michelle?" she asked as she approached the table.

"That's us," said the taller of the blondes. "I'm Michelle."

"So I'm obviously Emma," the other said with a forced laugh. She was the one who was probably closer to thirty.

"Have a seat," Michelle said. "We didn't know what rules agents had while on duty, but we got a glass for you, too."

Had it been any earlier in the day, Mackenzie would have passed. But seeing as how it was after nine at night and the only stop she had after this was back to the motel, she allowed herself a drink. She poured from the pitcher, giving the two women a chance to get accustomed to the idea that they were sitting in a bar with an FBI agent.

"So I'm going to ask some questions that might surprise you," Mackenzie said. "I would really appreciate your candor and keep it quiet for now. In a small town like this, gossip spreads fast and I'm afraid that anything that might get out could hinder the investigation."

"Investigation," Emma said. "Do they typically do investigations into suicides?"

"We do when there are strange circumstances surrounding the suicide," Mackenzie said.

"Good," Michelle said. "Because there's no way in hell Malory killed herself."

"What makes you so sure of that?"

"Well, it was against her beliefs for one," Emma said. "Malory had some pretty strong beliefs. She wasn't like a holy roller or anything like that but she prayed and went to church on most Sundays. I know for a fact that she was vehemently against suicide."

"That's right," Michelle said. "Not only that, but that damn bridge scared her."

"Was Malory afraid of heights?" Mackenzie asked.

"No, not that I know of. But she was a bit of a sissy. All of those local ghost stories about the bridge being haunted by the people that had killed themselves on it spooked her. I'm sure she didn't really believe it, but still...she was a big baby about that sort of thing."

The two friends shared a longing stare before Emma grabbed her glass and drained the remainder. She immediately refilled it, bringing the pitcher to within about half a cup of being empty.

"Do either of you know if she had any enemies? Even people who might have been envious of her for any reason?"

61

"No," Michelle said. "And that's the thing that confuses me. I can tell you without a doubt that she did not willingly jump off of that bridge. So someone had to have taken her there against her will. The only person I ever heard her speak ill about was her father. He was a bastard. Even though Malory never actually said so, I've always thought there was some sort of sexual abuse in their history."

As Emma nodded, Mackenzie sipped from the beer. It was a little flat and of the generic light beer variety; not close to her preference, but the feel and taste of it were welcome in the tense and awkward space of this backwoods bar.

"What was a typical night out for the three of you like?" Mackenzie asked.

"Like this, only happier," Emma said. "Sometimes there would be guys that would buy us drinks. Mostly guys from high school that never left town—just like us, I guess. But nothing bad, you know? Despite what you might think about Kingsville and towns like it, there aren't many creeps. Old men don't try to hit on us. Most of them know our dads, anyway. There's usually not a whole lot of trouble around here, you know? I think I've seen *two* fights in this bar and I've been coming here a lot since I was twenty-one."

"How about Mike Case? Either of you know him?"

Michelle frowned and sipped from her beer. Emma chuckled a bit and looked away. "Oh yeah," Michelle said. "He and I have an off-again-on-again thing. It's been off again for a pretty good while now."

"I'm learning that he has a reputation," Mackenzie said.

"He does," Michelle said. "He sleeps around and starts shit with anyone that dares to bother him. But he's not....well, he wouldn't be a suspect. Everything he does is all a show. It's to distance himself as far away from his dad as he can. That kind of guy."

"Did he know Malory?"

"Not well," Emma said. "Just in passing. And enough for Malory to tease Michelle about hooking up with him all the time."

"So let's assume there *was* someone else involved," Mackenzie said. "Is there anyone at all either of you would think might do such a thing?"

Both women shrugged at the same time, almost in a choreographed move.

"I really can't think of anyone," Emma said. "Honestly."

"Yeah," Michelle agreed. "If there was someone else involved, I don't know that it would have been anyone from around here."

It was a suspicion that Mackenzie had started to ponder on her drive back from DC. She was hoping it was not the case because when the suspect pool opened up to someone from out of town, finding a solution became infinitely harder.

Hearing it from these two women who not only knew the town intimately, but Malory Thomas as well, made Mackenzie realize it was actually very likely that she might be looking for an outsider after all. It felt certain enough in that moment for Mackenzie to raise her glass to her mouth and take two big gulps from her beer as if trying to wash the thought away.

CHAPTER FIFTEEN

Maybe it was the stress and frustration of what was going on with Ellington, or perhaps it had something to do with feeling that the case was beginning to get away from her, but when Mackenzie got back to the motel she wished she had downed a few more beers at Road Runner's. If nothing else, it might help her to sleep easier.

She set up her laptop, knowing that there was very little she could do. She had a few people back in DC doing background work, trying to find links between all of the suicide victims but really homing in on Kenny Skinner and Malory Thomas. There was nothing much she could do on her end until tomorrow morning when she met with Sheriff Tate and Deputy Andrews.

She climbed into bed just past eleven but knew right away that she would not be falling asleep anytime soon. Her mind kept going back to Ellington and what he was going through. More than that, she was starting to understand that she was beginning to rely on him far too much. She wasn't sure how she felt about this; it was one thing to admit that you were in love with someone but a totally different thing altogether to admit that being apart from a specific person made you feel lonelier than you ever had before. And if she was being honest with herself, that's where she was headed—if she wasn't there already.

That would at least explain why she had felt so off…so *different*…on both occasions when she had come to Kingsville. It was her first case without him by her side since they had become involved and quite honestly, it felt too different. She wasn't sad, per se, but she did feel incomplete.

This is pathetic, she thought to herself while she was lying in bed, wishing sleep would come quickly. *I sound like the end of* Jerry Maguire *and I am starting to hate myself a little bit. Maybe I was so upset about the sexual harassment allegations not because I was disappointed in him, but because I was angry—angry that something dumb he had done in his past can so heavily affect what he and I have now.*

And that's what scared her the most. It's what made a very small part of her wonder if she should call things off with him. He made her feel safe, secure, and loved. But depending on him so heavily made her wonder how it might affect her judgment in the future and, as a result, her career. While she had never considered herself a feminist, she also had never seen herself as the type of woman who would ever need a man to make her life feel complete.

Yet here she was…

The thoughts felt heavy, like stones sitting on her chest. But those same stones helped her to eventually sink into sleep even when she was intimately aware of the absence of Ellington on the other side of the bed.

***

The cornfields were such a staple of her dreams that it felt like stepping into a theme park. She knew what to expect along the edges and main walkways but it was the things that existed within the field that she knew could ruin her. So when she started to dream of those Nebraska cornfields for only the second time since bringing her father's murderer to justice, she did so with a reluctant familiarity.

She was standing in the middle one of the rows, looking out toward a horizon painted with the reds and golds of sunset. There was blood on the stalks and faint footprints along the row. She followed the footprints, feeling an impending sense of danger almost right away. She went for her Glock but discovered that it wasn't there. In fact, the holster wasn't there—nor were her pants.

She was standing naked in the cornfield, a fact that brought Malory Thomas to her sleeping mind. The dirt was warm under her bare feet, reminding her of sand along the beach. She walked along the row, gazing ahead toward the fractured light of the sunset through the stalks. She took two steps, then three—and then the ground changed.

The stale dirt changed into wood, the wooden planks of some type of walkway. The cornfield all around her was the same with this one exception. She walked on, the cornstalks nudging at her as she passed. The wood was smoothed with age under her feet and as she looked around, she saw that there was no dirt beyond the wooden planks, just cornstalks that seemed to grow out of the planks. Mackenzie stopped walking, gently pulled a few of the leaves from the stalks aside, and looked out.

On the other side of two rows of stalks, there was open air. There was a drop-off. And waiting at the bottom was the dried riverbed beneath the Miller Moon Bridge.

She was standing on the bridge. No rails, just cornstalks from some other terrible moment in her life, as if all the memories she had made were somehow knitting themselves together to haunt her.

Startled, she cried out and took a few steps back. She briefly felt the stalks on the other side of the bridge at her back but by then it was too late. Her retreating left foot stepped out into open space as she stepped backward. She fought for balance but had already lost the battle with gravity.

She was falling. Both of her feet went cartwheeling in the air. And as she fell, the bridge and the cornstalks growing fainter as she dropped, she saw the dangling shape of Malory Thomas on the side of the bridge. Malory was screaming for help but all Mackenzie could do was scream right back in response.

She shouted, waiting for the impact, waiting to strike and feel that last blast of pain from the rocks at the bottom of the bridge.

Her ears were filled with ringing, rhythmic and far away, something familiar to follow her down.

She jerked awake and realized that the ringing sound was the ringing of her cell phone.

She grabbed her phone and checked the call and the time all at once. It was 4:50 in the morning and the call was from Sheriff Tate.

"This is Agent White," she answered.

"You're back in town, right?" he asked her.

"Yeah, at the motel. What's up?"

"We got another body. You think you can come check it out?"

She saw the strange hybrid bridge from her dream and the thought of looking down from it jarred her. She tried to tell herself it was simply because she was not fully awake yet.

"Yeah. Are you guys already there, at the bottom of the bridge?"

"Well, no. This one isn't at the bridge. You know where the water tower is?"

"Yes." She had seen it on both passes into town and made arrangements to be there as soon as she could. She splashed some cold water on her face and got dressed as quickly as she could. And even as she pulled her car out of the motel parking lot five minutes later, she could not shake the feeling from her dream—an intense and guttural sensation of falling.

CHAPTER SIXTEEN

Mackenzie was fortunate enough to fall in behind a police cruiser on its way to the tower. With the twists and turns of the country back roads, there was no way she would have found it as easily as she had assumed. She followed the cruiser down a road that was very similar to the one that led to Miller Moon Bridge, only instead of gravel, this one turned off onto a dirt road. A few hundred feet down, they passed through a chain-link fence, the gate of which had already been opened.

She drove through the dust kicked up by the car ahead of her until it came to a stop. The water tower stuck up out of the pre-dawn darkness, as if welcoming them.

When she got out of the car, she saw that the patrol car she had followed in had been driven by Officer Roberts. He gave her a nod of acknowledgment as they walked together past two other police cars.

The only other police on the scene were Sheriff Tate and Deputy Andrews. They were standing with a man in a polo shirt and a pair of battered khakis. The lone pickup truck parked by the patrol cars bore a County Maintenance decal on its door. Mackenzie assumed he was a county employee, probably responsible for opening up the gate she had driven through.

Mackenzie could already see the shape of the body, lying directly below the water tower. The scene was a little less formal than the Kenny Skinner scene beneath the bridge; the only lights being used were the headlights from the maintenance truck and the sheriff's car.

"We have an ID yet?" Mackenzie asked.

"Her name is Maureen Hanks. Thirty-two. We haven't told anyone just yet, not even the family. She's got a three-year-old daughter."

Saying this seemed to choke Tate up a bit. Cautiously, Mackenzie approached the body. It wasn't in as bad a shape as Kenny's body. From the looks of it, the only visible injury was a broken neck. There was *some* blood, haloed around her head. Mackenzie imagined that once the body was moved, there would be much more.

"How was she discovered?"

Sheriff Tate only frowned in response, letting Deputy Andrews answer. "Her husband reported her missing at about one in the morning," he said. "We had an officer drive around looking for her...honestly, nothing too engaged. There are rumors about her and another man, though I don't know that they've reached her husband. So the officer went around town, looking for some of the spots we've busted teens for parking and messing around. He found her body here a little after four in the morning...a little over an hour ago."

"Any idea who the lover might be?" Mackenzie asked.

"Well, it's all speculation," Andrews said, "but all signs point to a guy named Bob Tully. He's got a clean record, a pretty good guy if you want to know the truth. Well, if you take out the whole part about having sex with another man's wife, I suppose."

Mackenzie looked away from Maureen Hanks's body and started to slowly circle the water tower. She wasn't sure what she was looking for just yet, outside of an obvious way to get to the small walkway that circled the top of the tower.

She found that access point on the backside of the tower. It was a thin ladder made of metal rails. It seemed study enough, though a bit narrow. The idea of having to climb it repeatedly for a job made her stomach lurch a bit. She heard Tate approaching, shining a flashlight upward for her. The county maintenance man was walking behind him, keeping a distance as if he really wanted nothing to do with it.

"So this ladder is just here, in the open, all the time?" she asked.

"Yeah," the maintenance man said. "It's bolted to the side of the supports that hold the tower up. It stops up there on the platform."

"To your knowledge, has there ever been trouble with people going up there to just goof off?"

"Not that I'm aware of," he said. "That gate you came through is always locked. Now, if we're being honest, there *is* a back way to get to it." He pointed to the left, where a strip of trees was shrouded by the night. "About fifty yards beyond that grove of trees and brush, there's an old field. Used to be a hay field, I think. There's then a series of old hunting and logging roads that wind around for a ways until you get back to the main roads. If someone *really* wanted to get to the tower, they could come that way, through those trees."

Mackenzie walked underneath the tower. She could feel the immense size and weight of it over her head. As she looked upward, Tate followed her gaze with his flashlight beam. As the light trailed up the thick supports, Mackenzie pointed.

"Right there," she said. "The graffiti. See it?"

Tate brought the light back down and focused it in on where someone had scrawled some markings with spray paint. They walked closer and saw that there were other markings, too. Some were scratched in with a knife, others scrawled in marker. *Dennis loves Amy. For a good time call 555-2356, ask for Paul's MOM. NIN forever! ANARCHY!*

There was more, but it was all the same—almost copied and pasted from any other graffiti site. Crude drawings of genitals, off-the-cuff remarks about women.

"You ever busted anyone in town for graffiti?" Mackenzie asked Tate.

"Yeah, actually," Tate said. "It's this twenty-year-old guy that tagged one of the old grain silos out on the other side of town a year or so ago. He's a little firebug, too. Starting fires in open fields, setting old dumpsters on fire behind the convenience store, things like that."

"Well, the graffiti is proof that at least a few people are either scaling the gate along the road or coming in the back way. And if someone came here to throw this woman off of it, it would have to be the back way most likely."

"Do you even think there's a chance it was a suicide?" Tate asked.

"No. Not based on what I've learned from the details that are slowly emerging in the cases of Malory Thomas and Kenny Skinner."

"But why the water tower?" the maintenance man asked.

"Because the killer has likely seen that you guys are keeping the road to Miller Moon Bridge under a watchful eye. He had to find somewhere else to go."

"But that raises another question altogether," Tate said.

"It does," Mackenzie agreed. "Why does he need a high place? If he wants to kill these people, why doesn't he just do it some simpler way? Why take the time to cart them out to the bridge or to somehow force them to climb this ladder?" she said, nodding toward the ladder that led up to the platform that encircled the water tower.

With a slightly queasy feeling in her stomach, she walked over to the ladder. She looked up and tried to imagine someone forcing her to climb it. What would it take? A gun to her back? Some threat of bodily harm?

"Sheriff, do you have a kit in your car to dust this thing for prints?"

"We do. One second."

While Tate went back to his car and spoke with Deputy Andrews for a few moments, Mackenzie went back to the body of Maureen Hanks. She was fully clothed, and aside from the discoloration and swelling around her obviously broken neck, she saw no signs of any sort of a struggle. She realized that she'd once again have to be patient and await autopsy results. More waiting, more back and forth with DC, trying to figure out an avenue.

Or I could just stay here for a while, she said. *I've got the man that was sleeping with her to talk to and then there's the local arsonist Tate mentioned. There's plenty to do here—plenty of reasons to keep me away from DC while this thing with Ellington settles down.*

Tate and Andrews came back over with an evidence kit while Roberts and the maintenance employee remained back at the cars. Mackenzie stepped aside, letting the officers do their job. She watched as Andrews expertly brushed for prints. Andrews did the work, testing the first four rungs of the ladder for prints. When he was done five minutes later, he gave her a shrug.

"We'll run these, but I wouldn't expect too much. We know Maureen's prints will be on it and probably at least one or two county employees'."

"It's at least something," Mackenzie said, again looking up the ladder. She then looked at Tate and asked: "Can I borrow that flashlight?"

He handed it over to her and looked instantly up the ladder. Apparently, he knew what she had in mind. "Want a second pair of eyes?"

"Thanks, but I think I'm okay. How far up is it?"

"I believe it's just over one hundred and thirty feet," Andrews said.

Honestly, she rather *did* want someone else to accompany her. But the thought of being up there on an already tight space with another person made her apprehensive.

Mackenzie tucked the flashlight in the pocket of her jacket. It was a larger Maglite, the back end of it sticking out of her pocket. Slowly, she started climbing up. She was fine for the first few rungs but once she saw the ground slowly disappearing from beneath her, she started to get shaky. Her fear of heights wasn't an intense one but it was strong enough to give her pause.

She kept her eyes focused in front of her, watching her hands as they went from one rung to the next. Sensing the legs and supports of the water tower close by helped to ground her but she still felt almost stranded as she made her way up.

She finally made it to the platform, having to pull herself up by metal handles along the edges of the safety railing that bordered the platform. She stepped as close as she could to the water tank, willing herself not to look down. She trailed the light all around the platform. It was dirty and scuffed up but unobstructed. She walked beyond the pump and valves along the rear end of it and continued the complete circuit around the platform.

She wasn't sure what she was looking for. Maybe nothing…maybe she just wanted to get a feel for what it would be like to be standing on this thin space, knowing someone who was with you meant to do you harm.

But more importantly than that, she thought, *what sort of headspace do you have to be in to have the desire to bring someone up here with the express intent of pushing them over the side?*

Finally, she allowed herself to look down over the rib-high safety rail. She saw the cars, shooting their headlights forward. The shadows of Tate and Andrews stretched out into the darkness. The maintenance employee and Officer Roberts looked like little action figures stacked together by the cars.

And then there was, of course, Maureen Hanks. Her body looked almost like part of the landscape. If not for the angles of her knees and elbows, one might think someone had discarded some garbage down below from this height.

Maybe that's an MO for the killer. From up here, it all seems small. Small and very insignificant.

It was an eerie feeling to have while standing on a thin strip of iron and metal while one hundred and thirty feet in the air. But at the same time, she could not deny the feeling that she was somehow superior over what she saw down below while standing so high up. It was, she thought, exactly the sort of feeling a killer might need to touch upon to find a sense of self-worth.

It was this slight etching of a profile that gave her the courage to slowly walk back around to the ladder. But the moment her foot went out into open space for the rung, she thought of her dream, of how being claimed by gravity was just one slippery rung away.

CHAPTER SEVENTEEN

Mackenzie allowed Sheriff Tate to ride along with her as they went to the address of Lawrence King. King was the twenty-something they had mentioned as being something of the town's resident arsonist. On the way to King's mobile home, Tate did his best to describe the suspect without being too derogatory.

"He's not mentally disabled or anything," Tate explained. "But he's just...*slow*. I don't know how else to explain it. You talk to him and he's just not all there."

Mackenzie nodded because she had seen the type before. Usually people who lived with a bent toward the destruction of only small things (rather than the kinds of massive destruction that came to mind when thinking of terrorists), had a vacant look in their eyes. They spoke like they were calculating each word, perhaps making sure they weren't giving anything away—making sure they weren't opening a doorway into vulnerability.

They arrived at the trailer park where King lived at 6:12 in the morning. The place was motionless with the exception of a single work truck rolling out of the trailer park entrance and onto the main road. Tate was driving and Mackenzie noted that he wasn't having to check a database or call for an address; he knew where Lawrence King lived, perhaps by reputation.

Tate parked the car in front of a trailer that was the very epitome of a mobile home. There was a slightly lopsided porch that covered the first half of the trailer. A glass screen door was slightly ajar, covering a front door that looked like it might be made out of cardboard. As they walked up the rickety porch steps, Mackenzie noted two cans of spray paint, discarded and on their sides in one corner of the porch. She also saw a few empty soda cans, the bottoms hollowed out and adorned with obvious burn marks.

Tate knocked on the door rather hard. The entire trailer seemed to shake with the force of it.

"Is there any chance of danger here?" Mackenzie asked.

"Highly doubtful," Tate said. "I don't know that he'd have the capacity to actually attack someone. But really...now that I think about it, pitching people off of high places might be sort of up his alley. You might get what I mean when you speak with him."

72

There was still no answer, so Tate knocked one more time. She could tell that he was getting irritated. His posture and behavior—in addition to the fact that he had instantly knew where King lived—made Mackenzie wonder if Tate had been out here a few times in the past. It made sense if King had a history of arson.

After another thirty seconds, Lawrence King answered the door. He was a scrawny man with shaggy black hair, looking to be in his early twenties. He was dressed only in a pair of jogging shorts, probably quickly thrown on when he had been jerked out of sleep by a knocking at his door. It was clear that he was not fully awake, squinting out to them with narrowed eyes even though the sun was not yet fully shining in the morning sky.

"What?" King asked, apparently not too concerned with the fact that there was a cop at his front door first thing in the morning.

"Lawrence, I'm sorry to wake you up so early this morning, but I need to ask you some questions."

"Okay."

It was clear that they were not going to be invited in. It was also clear to Mackenzie that Lawrence King was not a man of many words. And just based on the way he handled the situation, she didn't think he was doing it out of any sort of disrespect. He was still half asleep and honestly didn't seem to even find the situation all that strange.

"Where were you last night?" Tate asked.

"After work I came here and got a bite to eat. After that I went over to Mike Tharpe's and played some poker."

"How long were you there?"

King shrugged. He seemed to be coming around now. The multiple questions also seemed to bring a bit of alarm into his expression. "Maybe two or three hours. It was around eleven or so when I got back home."

"Did you go right to sleep when you got here?"

"No. I was up for a while. Watched some stuff on the Internet."

Mackenzie was watching King's face the entire time, trying to get a read on him. When he gave his answer about watching something on the Internet, she was certain he was being honest. He looked to her very quickly and then to the boards of the porch. He was embarrassed to admit it, meaning that he *had* watched something on the Internet. Probably pornography if his guilty expression was any indicator.

Tate looked back at her, as if asking if she wanted a crack at him. She waited for King's gaze to come back up and meet them.

73

When it did, she asked: "How many people were playing poker last night?"

King took a moment to think it out. "Started with six of us. But then Jimmy Hudson lost fifty bucks on one hand and got pissed. He called everyone names and then left. The rest of us rode it out, though."

"You come out to the better?" she asked.

"Yeah. By only ten bucks. But that's better than nothing."

"Who else was playing poker with you?"

King gave the names without any hesitation. It was evident that he understood that they suspected him of something. He had quickly gone from sleepy one-word answers to lengthier explanations.

"Mr. King," Mackenzie asked, "do you know a woman by the name of Maureen Hanks?"

"I know who she is, but I don't know her well. She's a little older than me, I think. Graduated like three or four years ahead of me."

"How about her husband? Do you know him?"

"I did in high school. Pretty good guy. Why? Something wrong?"

"No, not at all," Tate said. "We've just been investigating something this morning. Thanks for your time, Lawrence. And look…I'm going to need you to give me your word that this conversation stays between us. Okay?"

King nodded. "Take care, Sheriff."

With that, Tate started down the porch. Mackenzie was taken aback by the quick departure, but she was fine with it. She didn't have any other questions and had already made up her mind anyway.

Back in the car, Tate turned the key and backed out of the dirt driveway. "Thoughts?" he asked.

"I think he's innocent. I also think whatever he watched online last night was embarrassing to him."

"Same here," Tate said. "His face got a little red, didn't it? Anyway…the names of the guys he played poker with…I know all of them. They're a good enough group of guys, I suppose. I'll follow up and make sure Lawrence was indeed there but I'm expecting to find he's telling the truth. You have to remember, I've questioned him at least three times about small arson claims and marking public property up. He's a shitty liar. And what I saw this morning…he wasn't lying."

Mackenzie nodded. She felt sure that Lawrence King was not their man, either. And even if they turned out to be wrong, they'd know within an hour at most, once Tate checked with the other poker players.

It was hard to see this as a dead end, seeing as how there was no real clear path in sight in the first place. Mackenzie felt that if they were going to get any kind of valuable information, it would come from Bob Tully, the man Maureen had been sleeping with on the side.

While she had played no hand in the unfolding of the Kingsville PD's schedule, she thought they were doing a fine job, all things considered. During their visit to Lawrence King, two officers had been on the way to the Hanks residence to inform her husband that Maureen's body had been found. For the sake of decency and the risk of defaming Maureen's character any further, they had decided to wait a few hours before calling Bob Tully. Of course, they wanted to speak with him before the news spread like wildfire around the town.

She listened to sporadic conversations between Tate and his men on the CB radio and via cell phone as they made their way from the trailer park to the station. She could sense the small-town feel of their department in these conversations, especially from the woman at the dispatch desk. When she spoke over the CB radio, Mackenzie could hear the pain in her voice, trying to restrain the emotion that came with the fact that a woman she had known on a first-name basis was dead—that she had likely been murdered.

And while she listened to this, Mackenzie's mind flashed back to the moment where she had stood along the platform on the water tower. She tried to hone back in on the feeling of being above it all, of being at one of the highest points in Kingsville and the sense of being able to squash everything beneath her.

It was an odd feeling, one that was very much unlike her. But at the same time, she felt like there was something there...maybe something she was missing.

The notion would not leave her alone and was still nagging at the back of her mind when Tate pulled them into the parking lot of the Kingsville PD. And even though the sun had properly claimed it spot in the sky, she still couldn't help seeing that pre-dawn darkness below her, waiting to pull her down into a free fall.

CHAPTER EIGHTEEN

At the station, Maureen Hanks had been added to the list of people who had died on Miller Moon Bridge. While she had not died as a result of a fall from the bridge, her death was being compared to the others because she had fallen from a great height to her death. There were already three cops searching through records and their database to try to find connections between Maureen and any of the other victims.

Surprisingly, they had already found one. Officer Roberts presented it to Sheriff Tate and Mackenzie when they came in.

"Seems Maureen and Malory served on some sort of kids' program at Kingsville Baptist church two summers ago," he said. "Beyond that, there's no connection between the two. It is funny, though, that Bob Tully was the guy who had been hired to mow the grounds and the cemetery that summer."

It was a flimsy lead but at least it gave them a deeper well to mine from if things got really dry. Mackenzie could only imagine the painstaking task of finding out what kids attended the summer program. And then getting their parents' names and maybe even the names of anyone else who had a hand in the summer program.

That would be a nightmare even with DC resources, she thought as she headed for the conference room. *Let's just hope it doesn't come to that.*

She found a pot of coffee filled to the top in the back of the conference room. She helped herself as Tate and Andrews filed in behind her. Andrews was on the phone with someone, setting up a meeting. When he got off, he looked like was getting a little sick. She could only imagine what the turmoil in a small town like Kingsville must be like when there is no doubt at all that there's a killer lurking around.

"That was Bob Tully," Andrews said. "I told him we needed to speak with him as soon as possible, but didn't give a reason. He's headed over right now."

"How did he respond?" Mackenzie asked.

"He was alarmed. He asked if it was about his mother. She's been ill for the last few weeks but refuses to take it easy. When I told him it was not about her, he seemed fine. Curious, sure, but he didn't try to get out of it."

"What do we do if it's not him?" Roberts asked.

"We can't jump to that just yet," Mackenzie said, thinking of the nightmare scenario of having to dig into the most minuscule of leads like the summer program that connected Maureen Hanks and Malory Thomas. It was quite infuriating because Mackenzie felt that with such a small town, the connections between people would be much easier to uncover.

"Then where do we jump?" Andrews asked.

"We don't," Tate said, taking the words right out of Mackenzie's mouth.

"Has anyone ever fallen from that water tower before?" Mackenzie asked.

"No," Roberts said. "We had someone double-check on that this morning. There's nothing like that. Nothing has ever happened out there that we know of."

"So the bridge and then the water tower," Tate said. "Why the heights?"

"I'm trying to piece that together myself," Mackenzie said. "The killer is either very respectful of heights, like an adrenaline junkie that gets off by sky diving or bungee jumping, or maybe the victims themselves are scared of heights."

"That's a good point," Tate said. "Roberts, can you and a few others look into that? Look into records, call family and friends. I know it won't be fun but it's all we have for right now."

Roberts did not look happy about the task but he gave a quick nod and left the conference room.

"So what do we do for now?" Andrews asked.

"We wait on Bob Tully," Mackenzie said, sitting down with her coffee. She looked to the conference room door as if willing him to show up.

***

Bob Tully showed up eight minutes later. He was dressed for work, headed to his job at the small lumber yard ten miles outside of town. He wore a plain button-down shirt that had seen sweat and stains in its lifetime. He also wore a pair of faded denim pants and a pair of old tattered work boots. When he was escorted into the conference room by Deputy Andrews, he looked genuinely confused.

Confusion seemed to turn into worry when Andrews closed the conference room door and he found himself standing in a room with the county deputy, sheriff, and a woman he had never met.

"I won't even lie," Tully said. "You guys have got me a little scared."

"We don't think there's any need to be," Sheriff Tate said. "Go ahead and take a seat, Bob."

Bob did as asked, pulling up a seat to the conference room table. Andrews also sat down, occupying the final seat.

"First and foremost," Tate said, "I'd like you to meet Agent White from the FBI. She's in town looking into some of the terrible things that have happened lately. I assume you've heard about Malory Thomas and Kenny Skinner by now?"

"I have," Tully said, eyeing Mackenzie suspiciously.

"We've brought you in because of another body that was found this morning," Mackenzie said. She was interjecting sooner rather than later to try to gauge his facial expressions and his response to an outsider who might seem to suspect him of a crime. So far, he seemed to be far too concerned to register much of anything else.

"Who?" Tully asked.

It was Tate who answered, giving the name in a way that insinuated he *knew* the name would mean something to Tully. "It was Maureen Hanks."

Mackenzie actually saw the color drop out of his face. She also saw that his eyes instantly started to brim with tears but he was doing his very best to fight them back.

"We called you in," Tate went on, "because we're aware of a rumor that has been circulating around town for a few months now. A rumor about you and Maureen."

Bob said nothing at first. One tear managed to slip down and he wiped it away from his face quickly.

"It's okay," Mackenzie said. "Mr. Tully, here's the deal. We have no intention at all of making your affair—if there *is* one—public. Given that Mrs. Hanks has just died, there is no benefit to smearing her name. However, if there was indeed something going on with the two of you, you might very well be our best source of information."

"You think I killed her?"

"I didn't even remotely say that," Mackenzie said.

"She's right," Tate said. "Bob...you need to tell us right now. Was there something going on between you and Maureen?"

"Yeah," he said, the word coming out like a gasp of breath.

"For how long?"

78

"I don't know. Five, six months maybe."

"Did you see her last night?" Mackenzie asked.

"Yeah."

"What time of the day was this, and what did you do?"

Some of the color had come back into Bob's face now. There was red in his cheeks, almost the same color she'd seen rise up in Lawrence King's cheeks less than an hour ago. She almost pitied him for a moment. It was clear that he was not the type who was going to boast about his conquest of a married woman. She thought he looked pretty miserable, actually.

"We met at the turn-off road off of Briar Road," he said. "We used that spot a lot. She'd park the car just off the side where it started to become a dirt road, you know? We met yesterday evening, just before nightfall. We got in my truck, went further down the road to where the field is, right there where you can see the water tower. And really, I'd rather not spell out what happened then."

"And we won't make you," Mackenzie said. "However, please know that there's going to be an autopsy. So if you two had sex, it's going to be evident that she had been sexually active hours prior to hear death. If you had *unprotected* sex, it's going to be traced back to you within a day or so of the exam."

"Shit," he said, and this time a small sob came out.

"How long were you together?" Tate asked.

"I'm not sure. Maybe an hour. We met right before dark and it was pretty much completely night when I pulled back out to the dirt road."

"And what happened when you left there?" Mackenzie asked.

"I dropped her off at her car and left. It's the same way we've always done it."

"Did you see her get into the car?"

"No. I pulled off pretty quick. She...she sort of freaked me out last night. Made me think that if she knew we could get away with it, she'd keep going on with what we were doing. Me...I've been feeling guilty about it for a while now. I mean...she's got a kid. And...well, now she's *dead?*"

"Yes," Mackenzie said. "Her body was found at the bottom of the water tower. Her neck was broken and all signs point to her falling from the top of the tower."

"You think she jumped?" Bob asked.

"Do *you?*"

He shook his head right away. "No. No, not Maureen. She might have had some guilt and bad feeling about what we were doing, you know? But no. She wasn't the suicidal type. She loved her family, as weird as that sounds, considering who you're talking to. Her little girl was the world to her."

"Forgive me for asking," Tate said, "but do you have any proof of your whereabouts after you dropped her off?"

"A few, I guess. I went by Pop's store and got a six-pack. Went home, drank a few beers and watched some TV. Pop would probably remember me getting the beer. There was no one in the store when I stopped by. Other than that, though…wait. I did make a phone call around ten or so."

"Who'd you call?" Tate asked.

"Sam Brooks. I'm trying to talk him into selling me one of his acoustic guitars."

"Did you call on your cell?" Mackenzie asked.

"Yeah," he said. He took out his cell phone, pulled up the call history, and showed it to them. The call had been placed at 10:07 and had ended at 10:12.

Mackenzie nodded. "I'll be honest with you, Mr. Tully. I don't think you did it. I really don't. But given your relationship with her and that you were likely the last person to see her alive outside of anyone who might have forced her to the top of that tower, we need to question you pretty thoroughly."

"So I'm a suspect?"

"Yes, but only by default."

"I'll help however I can," he said. "But I would really rather her husband not know about this."

"Did you use a condom?" Mackenzie asked.

"Yes."

"Then your name can probably be omitted entirely for now. Assuming you're innocent, of course."

Bob Tully nodded and Mackenzie felt like she was looking at a broken man. She wasn't sure if he'd felt anything for Maureen Hanks other than lust, but he was clearly hurt over the news of her passing.

She felt in her gut that Bob was innocent. But she also knew that if they didn't find a killer soon, or at least irrefutable proof that Bob was at home all night after the phone call about the guitar, he would probably spend the foreseeable future in this conference room or a holding cell somewhere.

I guess I need to see what I can do to make sure that doesn't happen, then, Mackenzie thought as she drained her cup of coffee.

CHAPTER NINETEEN

They ended up releasing Bob Tully for lack of real evidence, but a few formalities were set into place. He had been instructed not to leave town until the case was wrapped and, in secret, a cop was tasked with keeping surveillance on him just in case. Mackenzie looked over the brief report that had been drawn up in regards to the apparent murder of Maureen Hanks just to make sure all of her bases were covered.

Then, with no real avenue to pursue, she went back out to her car and headed toward the water tower. She found it much easier this time, approaching it from the same direction Bob and Maureen would have been coming the night before. She parked her car where she assumed Bob and Maureen had parked. The water tower was perhaps two hundred yards away, a faded white bulk in the distance.

Mackenzie got out of her car and walked to the grove of forest that separated the tired old field from the water tower. She had never been one to mind nature, but there was something about the isolated feel of Kingsville. She could only imagine what it must have felt like for Maureen Hanks as she had been led toward the water tower among these trees and brush at night.

She reached the clearing where the water tower stood and went back beneath it. She studied the graffiti and checked around on the ground for anything she might have missed the night before. She once again went to the ladder and climbed up. It was less stressful in the light of day, easier for her to convince herself that she did not have a fear of heights.

At the top, she looked down, trying to reconnect with that sensation she had felt last night—the sense of power, the sense of standing tall over everyone else.

She wondered if that's what was attracting the killer to these high places. Did he need to feel powerful? And if so, how did that tie in to his need to kill his victims?

No, that doesn't make sense, she thought. *If he needs the feeling of being over something, he'd likely also need it to get his victims to these high places. It's more likely that he's bringing the victims with him for a reason.*

81

"Because he doesn't want to be alone," she said out loud. It was an easy thing to consider; she had, after all, felt a pang of isolation by just walking to the water tower.

She shifted gears in her head, trying to see the points of view of both murder sites from someone who may fear the height rather than use it as a tool to fabricate a sense of power. Right away, it seemed to make sense. It could almost be like a sacrificial system, in a way. The killer takes the victims to these high places, probably meaning to kill them anyway, but why? It was a question that could have multiple answers but it also gave her at least some sort of motive, no matter how skewed.

Having a slight fear of heights made it easy for Mackenzie to identify with this probable motive. But she still knew nothing about the killer. She was going to have to speak to someone who knew a little more about specific phobias.

And just her luck, there just happened to be someone who could potentially help her less than five miles away.

***

Jan Haggerty hadn't sounded all that surprised when Mackenzie had called her and fifteen minutes later, when she answered Mackenzie's knock at her door, she looked nearly expectant. The next few moments were nearly a complete replay of what had occurred the first time Mackenzie had visited. They walked into the kitchen where Dr. Haggerty poured large cups of black coffee and then they entered her office.

"You know," Haggerty said, "I only heard about Maureen Hanks about fifteen minutes before you called."

"How did you hear so soon?" Mackenzie asked.

"Ah, the small-town grapevine. My mother-in-law called and said she thought I'd probably get a visit from that FBI lady again. I asked her why and she told me. And God only knows how she knew."

"And how did she know I paid you a visit earlier in the week in the first place?" Mackenzie asked.

Haggerty only shrugged as she sipped from her coffee. When she set it down, she said: "People are nosy around here. I'm afraid it's one of the many stereotypes about small towns that just happen to be true."

"Well, the reason I'm here again is because I was hoping you might know a thing or two about phobias—particularly a fear of heights."

82

"Fear of heights is known acrophobia," Haggerty said. "It comes down not even really to a basic *fear* of heights. It's more of a trust issue—trusting your own balance and that the thing you are standing on at such a height will not fail you."

"Do you know if it's just an instilled sort of thing, like something people either have or don't have? Or can a traumatic event maybe put it in you?"

"I'm sure both are true," Haggerty said. She considered something for a moment and then added: "I assume you think the murderer has some attraction or aversion to height, yes?"

"I do," she said. "And I was hoping you could help me figure out how someone like that would think. I assume that he's scared of heights and is using the murders as a way to overcome that fear."

"That's interesting," Haggerty said. "What led you to that conclusion?"

"Other than some sick fascination with control—which I haven't ruled out yet—there's simply no solid reason to choose throwing people from a great height as a means of killing them. It makes me think that he's taking these people to these heights because he's afraid to face them himself."

Haggerty nodded. "Interesting. So he *could* be pushing them off when he discovers that they are not helping him overcome his fear."

"Or when he *does* start to feel safer and sees them as disposable," Mackenzie added.

"If we *are* dealing with someone with these kinds of mental issues, there are a few basic things to consider," Haggerty said. "What's the source of his fear? Why has he chosen these people as his victims? Does he see them as some sort of link to his fear of heights?"

"So would you agree with me that the killer has a fear of heights rather that some sort of love for them due to a sense of power or control?"

"Yes, I believe so. Someone that was in it for the control aspect would likely not choose something as unpredictable as high places for the scene of the crime. Too much is taken out of their hands. There's too much unpredictability. And speaking of which…I wonder…can you tell me if Maureen Hanks was naked?"

"No, she was not."

"But Malory Thomas was, right? See…it makes me wonder if there is some sort of synaptic disconnect in the killer. A legitimate phobia is, at its base, just the body's arousal in a situation—not sexual in most cases, but just a heightened state of alert. When this kicks in, your nervous system floods your body with either the need to escape or the need to explore something further. It seems like our killer might land somewhere between those two."

"So if you had to place money on it, would you say the killer has some sort of mental detachment?"

"If he does, it's not going to be a severe one. Making a woman climb all the way to the top of that water tower requires patience, planning, and bravery."

"I was thinking the same thing," Mackenzie said.

"You know, I'm not an expert on phobias and I honestly don't know anyone that is. But I do know that there are support groups for this kind of thing all over the place. If you'll give me a second, I can probably find a business card for someone who runs one of these groups up near your neck of the woods."

"That would be perfect. Thanks."

Mackenzie sipped from her coffee as Haggerty stepped away elsewhere into the house. Mackenzie started to think about the kind of person who might feel that same sort of control and power she had contemplated while standing on the water tower. But it was more complicated than that; it also had to be someone who had a fear of such a height—and maybe, if she dared go a step farther, a respect and awe of that fear.

A few moments later, Haggerty appeared with the promised business card. She handed it to Mackenzie with a frown on her face. "I really wish I could do more to help."

"Nonsense," Mackenzie said. "You've been a tremendous help. Little things like this," she said, holding up the business card, "can usually be much more help that you'd expect."

"I hope so," Dr. Haggerty said. "When word *really* gets around as to what's been happening here in town, it's going to get crazy. People stop trusting each other. Friendships and family ties break down. It can get nasty in small towns like this."

"Well, let's hope we find our killer before it gets to that point," Mackenzie said.

Yet when she left two minutes later with nothing more than an old business card for her troubles, finding a killer seemed harder than ever.

CHAPTER TWENTY

Mackenzie was glad Kingsville was just over an hour away from DC; it made the back and forth monotony of it all much more bearable. She wasn't stranded like she typically was when she was on assignment elsewhere in the country. Because of the close proximity, it only took her forty-five minutes to get from Kingsville to Herndon, which would place her only twenty minutes away from DC when she was done.

The business card Haggerty had given her was for a man by the name of Oswald Gates. The card claimed he was an LPC specializing in "achieving peace and rest through group settings." He'd seemed agreeable enough on the telephone and although he had not maintained a phobia-based group in over a year, he jumped at the chance to meet with her.

His office was located in a small brick building right in the center of the city. When Mackenzie parked in front of it, she took the plain generic building for the sort of place that held AA meetings regularly, and where there were probably thrift sales or bake sales for local charities on the weekends. Perhaps a little unfairly, she figured it was the perfect place for people to gather to discuss their fears.

She entered the building and found that it smelled of Pine-Sol and strong coffee. She figured it was a community center of sorts, complete with a corkboard in the hallway with fliers, posters, and announcements about upcoming events. At the end of the hall, she found Oswald Gates's office. He was turned away from the door, digging through a battered gray filing cabinet. Mackenzie knocked on the door and Gates turned around to face her. He was a middle-aged African-American with a well-kept beard that covered most of his neck. He wore a pair of reading glasses that made his eyes look enormous.

"Hi, Mr. Gates," she said. "Thanks for meeting with me on such short notice."

"Of course," he said. "You know, Kingsville being so close, I've heard about those suicides. But I gathered on the phone with you that you think there might be something more to it?"

"That's the way it's looking," Mackenzie said. "As I said, I got your number from Jan Haggerty and she thought you might be able to offer some more insights into the mindset of someone who has a fear of heights."

"I can certainly try," he said. He slapped at a pile of files he had no doubt pulled from the filing cabinet behind him. "What would you like to know?"

"How much experience do you have with people with acrophobia?"

"A pretty good deal. Fear of heights is the most common fear among humans. It's so common that most people don't even think about coming to support groups for it because they think it's perfectly normal. I *have* worked with a few, though."

"Do you recall any who were aggressive? Do you find that aggressions or maybe even depression seems to be linked to a fear of heights?"

Gates took a moment to think about that and then shook his head. "No. Again, it's such a common fear that there's rarely anyone ashamed of it. Now you'll have people that get scared of heights even when they look down from the railing of their front porch and those are the types that might get embarrassed about the phobia. But no…as far as I know, based on my own experience and what I've read on the matter, aggression isn't a byproduct of acrophobia."

"Can you tell me maybe some of the things you *can* align with people with this fear?" Mackenzie asked.

"Yeah, it's pretty easy. I worked with one man for about six months because he knew he was headed into a career where he'd have to travel a lot. And the thought of getting on a plane didn't scare him at all. It was the chance that he might get a peek out of the window when they were in the air. He had night terrors about that for months.

"But even with him, it was an easy fear to navigate. I took him up to the roof of this building one day. Had a session up there. He was sweating it the whole time but when I showed him the fire escape out back—showed him that there was a safe way back to the ground—it helped. We then went on to another building and another until one day we went up to the clock tower near the center of town. Four stories tall and he was able to look down without losing his cool."

"So you think a gradual approach helps people overcome this fear?"

"Yes, and there are journals and studies on it that back it up."

"So based on all that you know, what do you think might cause someone who is scared of heights to forcibly take someone with them a high place?"

Gates frowned and said, "You mean like a bridge or a water tower?"

Mackenzie nodded. While she was not yet one hundred percent sold on the fact that the killer was afraid of heights, the look of grief on Gates's face made her lean even more toward it.

"It's hard to say," Gate responded. "Perhaps it's because it's a transfer of power or control. It's not unthinkable to assume that because being at those high places makes them feel frightened, having total control over someone at that scene might make them feel stronger. They could be using the victims as a source of power."

"You mean the mentality of 'I may be scared to be on this bridge, but I'm sure as hell in control of you so at least I'm in control of *something.*' Something like that?"

"Something like that, exactly," Gates said. "But I think if he's then taking it to the point of murder, it may be something more than just trying to get over a fear. I think in that instance, it's more about controlling the victim. He's trying to free himself of the fear by viewing these high locations as something other than a place that scares him. It seems like he's trying to make the place all about control."

"And although that's a messed up point of view, do you think someone could be successful at overcoming their fear in such a way?"

"I honestly don't know. That's so far beyond anything I've ever even pondered." He sighed and shook his head as if trying to shake the idea of it out of his mind. He then pushed the small pile of folders that had been sitting in front of him over to Mackenzie. "I looked through my files as far back as five years. Sorry to say this is all I could find for you."

Mackenzie flipped open the first file folder. The pile contained only seven and each one was very thick.

"What are these?" she asked.

"The notes and files I have on anyone who came through my door and had a legitimate fear of heights over the last five years. Like I said, there aren't many that seek actual help for it. And I really don't know if any of that will help. I figured maybe you'd find some sort of similarity between them all that might help."

"Yes, this is fantastic, thank you."

"I do ask that you not take them with you, though. Confidentiality and all. I might be willing to turn a blind eye if you wanted to take them to the print office at the other end of the hall and make copies, though."

"I think I'll just look them over right here if that's okay. It shouldn't take more than a few minutes."

"Help yourself," Gates said. "I need to go grab some papers from the print room, so make yourself at home. I'll be back in a second."

With that, Gates left the room and headed down the hall. Mackenzie wasted no time and dove right into the files. The files were quite thin, some only one page in content. But Gates took pretty good notes, detailing the person's thoughts and emotions as well as his own notes. She saw a lot of what they had just talked about but paid close attention to some of his bulleted notes.

One woman who had come in had even been afraid to get on elevators. For her, it wasn't the *sight* of heights that terrified her as much as the sensation of going up. She also saw a brief study of the man Gates had told her about—the man who had wanted to overcome his fear so he could take flights for work.

She spent five minutes looking through his notes, typing her own notes into her phone whenever she came across something noteworthy—and, quite honestly, there wasn't much.

That was, not until she got to the fifth folder.

This was the thickest folder by far. There were three pages of typed notes, a single sheet of Gates's notes, and then a dozen or so black-and-white photographs. She looked over the notes, seeing the story of a man named Tyler Black. He'd been terrified of heights as a child but had slowly gotten over them. As a teenager, he'd been arrested for indecent exposure, having sex on a condemned bridge just outside of New Jersey. He'd eventually made his way to Landover, Maryland, for a job and it had been there that the fear had hit him again. According to Gates's notes, Tyler had simply started having dreams about falling from tall buildings and of skydiving only to find that his parachute wouldn't open.

Mackenzie was most drawn to the fact that he had thought to have sex on a condemned bridge. Was it maybe in an attempt to overcome this fear? If so, it was very much like one of the pictures she and Gates had painted of her suspected killer just moments ago.

Gates entered the room behind her just as she reached the black-and-white photos in the back of the folder.

"Ah, that would be Tyler Black," Gates said.

Mackenzie was looking at the first picture as Gates reclaimed his seat behind the desk. It was a black-and-white photograph of a seemingly random building. The camera was angled up in order to capture the entire building. It was about five stories tall but was otherwise quite plain.

"What are these pictures of?" Mackenzie asked.

"Tyler had an interest in photography," Gates explained. "He did basic portraits, still life, that sort of thing. So one day I recommended that he start taking pictures of some of the high places that scared him. We talked it out and I thought it might help to overcome his fears if he could see the places he was scared of from a different perspective. To view them as a focal point of his art rather than a focal point of his fear."

"And did it work?" Mackenzie asked.

"It seemed to for a while but he stopped coming to see me right in the middle of it all. He called me one day and said he was doing much better. When I asked him to elaborate, I didn't get much."

Mackenzie nodded, impressed with Gates's approach. Seeing these high sights in a new way through the lens of photography was rather genius. She looked through the rest of the pictures, one of which was a shot of an old ironworks warehouse with a very tall exhaust tower in the rear. It was a fantastic picture, showing that Tyler Black had quite the eye for this sort of thing.

But it wasn't until she got to the fifth picture that the photographs really grabbed her attention.

"Mr. Gates…did you know this was in here?" she asked.

"What are you talking about?" he asked.

Mackenzie took one of the black-and-white photos out of the folder and slid it across the desk.

"I…I didn't even remember this one," Gates said, looking from the picture and then to Mackenzie. "Is this…?"

Mackenzie nodded, looking down at the picture as well.

"Yeah. It's the Miller Moon Bridge."

CHAPTER TWENTY ONE

While the discovery of Tyler Black's photo was a strong lead, Mackenzie did not feel that it was strong enough to warrant a call to the Herndon Police Department. Instead, she called Agent Harrison up in DC and asked for an information request. Five minutes later, she had Tyler Black's address as well as the address for his place of employment.

Since it was just after lunch time on a Thursday afternoon, Mackenzie took a gamble and decided to visit Tyler's place of employment—a construction company where he worked in the cabinet department. It was located in downtown Herndon, a nice office space that looked more like an upscale design firm than a construction company.

There were a few people behind desks, and one woman speaking very angrily on the phone. When the woman saw Mackenzie enter, she held up a finger, asking her to wait. Mackenzie did so, listening to the woman complaining for thirty seconds or so on the phone before finally hanging up and giving Mackenzie her attention.

"What can I do for you today?" the woman asked.

"I'm looking for Tyler Black," Mackenzie said.

The woman gave a chuckle and rolled her eyes. "Yeah, aren't we all?"

"I don't understand what you mean," Mackenzie said, doing her best to keep her cool.

"What I mean is Tyler quit earlier this week. Right in the middle of the day, he just told us to go fuck ourselves and stormed off. No one here has heard from him since."

"Did he not give any reason?"

"Nope. He did seem sort of unlike himself, though." The woman then eyed Mackenzie suspiciously. "Why are you asking?"

"I'm with the FBI," she said, pulling her badge and showing it to her. She had intended to keep it low key but the fact that her one solid lead had quit his job around the same time the body of Malory Thomas had been found was a little too strong to be overlooked.

"Oh," the woman said, dropping her attitude right away.

"So before he stormed out, was there anything at all about Tyler Black that alarmed you?" Mackenzie asked. "Anything that might have seemed out of the ordinary?"

"No, and that's the weird thing. Tyler was awesome. A great guy, a *cute* guy if I'm being honest. One of those men that always wanted to help people. Went out of his way to help sometimes. So yeah...when he walked out on Monday, it was a huge surprise."

"And you have no idea why he had the sudden change of attitude?"

"No. If you're looking for him, though, I can give you his address."

"No thank you," she said. "I've got it. Thanks for your time."

She turned away and made it only two steps back toward the door when her phone buzzed in her pocket. She pulled it out and saw that it was Harrison calling.

"What's up, Harrison?"

"You aren't going to believe this," Harrison said. "But after I got the addresses for Tyler Black, I went ahead and ran a full report request just in case. Turns out, he's not in Herndon."

"Yeah, I just found that out. So where the hell is he?"

"He's in jail in Baltimore County, Maryland. He's a new resident...just booked this morning."

"For what?"

"This is the smoking gun," Harrison said. "He was standing on the edge of the Francis Scott Key Bridge."

The timeline to all of this is eerie, she thought. *If he was booked this morning, that gave him plenty of time to drive from Kingsville, Virginia, to Baltimore, Maryland.*

As much as Mackenzie hated jumping to conclusions, this one was adding up to be a home run.

"Has he been processed yet?" she asked.

"I don't know. I can call and see."

"Do it. And no matter what the outcome, I need you to let McGrath in on this. I want Tyler Black in DC by the end of the day."

"You think he's the guy?"

She had to bite back a yes, not wanting to sound *too* certain. So instead, she answered with a much safer "We'll see."

***

The rest of the day seemed to lag on. Two hours after leaving Herndon, Mackenzie was back in her office in DC. She knew without a doubt that even if Tyler Black turned out to be the killer, she'd likely end up in Kingsville again. She was fine with that but still found herself trying to put the brakes on her certainty that this was the end of the case—that Tyler Black was the murderer.

When 4:15 arrived, Black was still in transit—half an hour later than had been estimated by the Baltimore County Sheriff's Department. That was fine with Mackenzie, though. She etched out a timeline of events in Kingsville on her dry erase board and then, beneath that, a timeline of events in Tyler Black's life along that same time frame. She had gotten bits and pieces of Black's story over the phone during the last few hours, and while she certainly didn't know all of the ins and outs, she knew enough to fill a timeline of the last five days.

And so far, it was not looking good for Mr. Tyler Black.

As she studied her timelines and went back through the files she had accumulated in Kingsville, Harrison poked his head in her open doorway. "He's here," he said. "They'll have him in an interrogation room within five minutes."

She nodded her appreciation as she took one more moment to look back through her files. She had never been one to make a suspect wait; she always thought the whole *let's make 'em sweat it out* was a bullshit tactic to make agents feel more in control of a situation than they actually were.

It was a sentiment that Ellington agreed with. And knowing that he'd be in just as big of a hurry as she was to start talking to Black made her miss him. But it was more than just pining for him and wishing that he was there with her. It came down to a comfort and familiarity that she had apparently been taking advantage of. They worked well together—both at work and at home—and it felt odd to not have him there with her as she left her office and headed downstairs to the interrogation rooms.

She found Harrington speaking with McGrath. Agent Yardley was there with them as well but she was speaking rapidly to someone on the phone at the other end of the hallway. There were two policemen from Baltimore County taking their leave, headed for the front office where they'd likely have to just sit and wait while the fate of their prisoner was decided.

"He just sat down in there," McGrath said as Mackenzie joined them.

"What sort of a mood is he in?" Mackenzie asked.

"The officers that brought him in say he's more scared than anything," Harrison said. "Maybe a little confused. But not at all volatile."

Mackenzie said nothing else. She collected her thoughts for a moment and then stepped inside. As always, the first thing she felt when entering an interrogation room was the camera in the far right corner, watching everything she did and recording everything she said. She then felt the eyes of the man sitting at the table, watching her closely as she stepped forward.

She sat down opposite him, not quite sure where to start. If he *was* the killer and was being motivated in some way by fear, she was sure she could get a confession out of him rather easily. But she also knew she had to remain as nonconfrontational as possible in order to get there.

"They tell me you were standing on the edge of the Francis Scott Key Bridge," Mackenzie said. "What were you doing there?"

"Just sort of looking out over the water," he said. His voice gave away his fear. He *was* very scared—whether because he had been caught or because of guilt, she didn't know.

"And standing on the edge is the only way to do it?" she asked. "Seems sort of dangerous. Especially for a man who's sought counseling for his fear of heights."

A flicker of surprise showed in his eyes, but it was quickly replaced by a resigned embarrassment. "How'd you know?"

"I spoke with Oswald Gates earlier today," she said.

"Oh," he said. And with that, she could see the cogs starting to turn in Black's head as he continued to try to figure out why he had been detained.

"I found the pictures you had taken pretty interesting," Mackenzie said. "Gates told me why you took them—trying to use photography as a way to sidestep your fears. Do you think it worked?"

"I thought it had," he said. "But…I don't know. There were days where I'd wake up with the fear all over again and it was worse than before. But…look…I'm confused as hell. I suppose I understand being arrested for stepping over to the side of the bridge and partially blocking traffic with my car. But…isn't this a bit much for such an offense?"

"What were you doing on the edge of the bridge?" Mackenzie asked. "Don't bullshit me. Just tell me like it is."

"Thinking about jumping," he said without any hesitation. "I'm tired of these fears, you know? It's not just heights. I get panic attacks in crowds…bad ones that make me feel like I have to puke. Some days it all just piles up together and it's a miserable feeling."

"Weren't you scared to be out there then, if you were scared of the height?"

93

"Yeah, I was terrified. But I figured if I could find the balls to jump then it's basically a big *fuck you* to the fear, you know?"

In the back of her mind, the certainty she'd had that Tyler Black was the killer slowly started to crumble. The killer was at least three victims in at this point—maybe more if the trail of bodies extended back farther than the past week. For someone with that sort of motivation, the thought of ending their own lives in the midst of their carnage was highly unlikely.

"When I met with Mr. Gates, I took a look through some of his files. I saw the pictures you took. One of them, I found very interesting. You see, I've spent the last several days in the little town of Kingsville, Virginia."

Black nodded. "That's where the Miller Moon Bridge is located. One of my pictures."

"That's right," Mackenzie said. "Can I ask why that particular bridge was of interest to you?"

"When I started trying to get over my fear of heights, I did some Googling. Looking for nearby bridges that weren't all that high—the more isolated and off the beaten path the better. I thought maybe I could ease myself into getting out of that fear by walking out over some of these lower bridges out in the middle of nowhere. Miller Moon Bridge came up. Cute little bridge, off in a really quiet place."

"It's also been the scene of two deaths in the course of the last five days," Mackenzie said.

She watched his face intently. She'd just pulled a pretty heavy trigger, solely to see his reaction, It was this reaction, she knew, that would help her identify whether or not he was guilty. And what she saw there was total surprise and a bit of shock.

"Suicides?" he asked.

She nodded. "At least, that's what they looked like. Digging a little deeper, it looks like they were murders."

The cogs in Black's head seemed to come to a screeching halt at this. "Is…is that why I'm here?"

"A trail of anecdotal evidence did lead us to you, yes. After speaking to a woman at your job and finding out that you left abruptly earlier this week right around the times the murders started made it look very bad. What was the episode at work about?"

"I stopped taking my anxiety meds. They made me hyper and dizzy, especially when we were busy at work. I was behind on deadlines, the fears were starting to creep back up, and I just snapped. It was the first of several things to happen that led me to the edge of the bridge today."

His expressions and lack of defensiveness had already made Mackenzie feel that he was not the killer. Still, there was protocol to be followed and loose ends to tie up.

"Where did you go when you left work that day?" she asked.

"I went back to my apartment. Took a nap, had a few beers."

"And how did you end up in Baltimore?"

"I'd been across the Francis Scott Key Bridge a few times before. It was familiar…bigger than anything else I'd tried using to overcome my fears, but…I don't know. I think even before I left Herndon for Baltimore I was thinking about jumping."

"Where did you stay in Baltimore these last few days?"

"A Holiday Inn."

"Do you have receipts? Any proof that you stayed around Baltimore these last few days?"

"I paid with a credit card so I can get receipts. And the only proof I have that I was in town the whole day are transactions I made. Lunch, taking in a movie, that sort of thing."

And that's the end of this lead, Mackenzie thought, relaxing back into her seat. "Thanks so much for your time, Mr. Black," she said as she got to her feet and headed for the door. "Sorry for the inconvenience."

She was out of the door and standing next to Harrison and McGrath before Black could respond. She felt foolish—maybe even a little lazy for having assumed that Tyler Black had been the answer to all of the questions she'd been accumulating since her first visit to Kingsville.

"He's not our guy," she said. "Some simple credit card traces over the last two or three days should prove it."

"He claims he was in Baltimore the whole time?" McGrath said.

"For at least the last two days. Which takes him completely out of Maureen Hanks's death and probably Kenny Skinner's, too."

"So where's that leave us?" McGrath said.

"Square one?" Harrison asked.

"Not quite square one," Mackenzie said. "But with all due respect, I just need to stay in Kingsville until this is done. Three deaths in the course of a week probably means the killer is there. My time is being wasted going back and forth."

She nearly added: *And without my partner, it's a little more grueling than usual.* But she kept her cool, swallowing the comment down.

"That's fine with me," McGrath said. "Just keep me posted on the phone. If you need any resources, keep calling Harrison. If you need a partner on this, I can also send him or Yardley."

"I appreciate that, but I think I'm good for now."

She was aware that she was sounding overconfident but the last thing she needed right now was a substitute partner. She'd do nothing but compare them to Ellington; she'd been forced into that position before and while it had worked out in the end, it had honestly been more trouble than it had been worth.

And speaking of trouble, she supposed she needed to make one last stop in DC before she headed back to Kingsville for the long haul. She needed to speak with Ellington and even then, as she made her way back to her office, she had no idea how the conversation would go or even where it needed to start.

CHAPTER TWENTY TWO

She heard the shower running when she entered her apartment. She also saw Ellington's gym bag at the front door, meaning that he had just gotten back from working out. She was glad to see that he was still staying active rather than moping around the apartment, wallowing in his bad fortune.

She let him enjoy his shower without bothering him. While she waited, she went into the bedroom and fired up her laptop. She had sent the case files from her phone to her personal folders on the FBI directory. She pulled them up, scrolling through them for anything she might have missed. Each case—Malory Thomas, Kenny Skinner, and Maureen Hanks—was cut and dry. The only thing that kept jumping out to her was the change in scenery. Of course, it made sense that the killer would change locations once the police had the Miller Moon Bridge under surveillance. It made her wonder if maybe they needed to call in the State PD to have eyes on any tall structure out in Kingsville. There weren't many, but they were numerous enough to the point that it would totally deplete Sheriff Tate's force if they went that route.

Behind her, she heard the shower turn off. She finished reading the current file she was on while the sounds of Ellington petering around in the bathroom came through the walls.

"Don't be alarmed," she called out. "But I'm here."

"Welcome back," he called from the adjoining bathroom. "Should I come out clothed or in the nude?"

"Clothed," she said. She sensed his attempt at humor but cut it off at the knees. Truth be told, she was still not entirely sure why the suspension was still bothering her. It made her feel juvenile and out of touch with reality. She could not go back to Kingsville with that feeling. She could not allow herself to be distracted by whatever toxicity existed between her and Ellington.

He did not respond to her following her comment, apparently hearing the seriousness in her tone. He appeared out of the bathroom two minutes later just as she was closing out of her files. He was dressed in a pair of jogging shorts and a T-shirt, his hair still wet from the shower.

"How goes the case?" he asked.

"It's still stalled," she said. "I'm heading back to Kingsville tonight."

"Got a lead to chase down?"

"No. I just want to be there in the morning rather than driving down early."

"You sure?" he asked, sitting on the edge of the bed. "It sure would be nice to have you here tonight. Unless you're still pissed at me about the suspension."

"I don't know *what* I'm pissed about," she admitted. "There's something off and I didn't feel it until the accusations against you popped up. But we need to figure it out now or it's going to get in the way of my work."

"Well, at the risk of sounding like a jerk, I think we found the problem right there in that statement," he said. "You're too worried about how the sins of my past are going to affect the way you approach your work now. So my question to you is whether you're more upset at me as your partner or me as your boyfriend."

"I think it's a bit of both. And quite frankly, I don't see how my putting the job ahead of you right now is a problem. You did something stupid in your past and it's coming back to bite you. There's absolutely no reason I should let it affect me and my work."

"But you are. And why is that?"

"Because I'm finding it hard to look at you the same way," she admitted.

"And is there any way to get over that? I mean…look, I understand at this point it's my word against hers but I hope you know me enough to know that my word is pretty solid."

"Yes, I do know that. I don't know…I think it's something deeper. Something I may not be ready to face just yet."

"And what's that?" he asked.

She knew the answer to it, but she wasn't ready to tell him just yet. But on the other hand, hadn't she come here to iron all of this out?

"What is it, Mackenzie?" he asked, reaching out and taking her hand. "Despite the suspension and despite the allegations against me, I'm still here. I'm still *me*."

"I know," she said. "Look…maybe I was wrong. Maybe this needs to wait until after the case. Because the more I think about it and the more we try to hash it all out, the more I start to see that it's all an issue with *me*. An issue *I'm* having."

"What issue?"

She hated that he was pressing her so hard but she knew it was out of love. That was why it was easier than she expected to finally give voice to it. "That I've become far too reliant on you. And that's new to me. I've never relied on anyone...never cared what anyone thought of me. And now so much of what I do—so much of my self-worth and my drive to be a better person—comes based on how I want you to perceive me. It's scary, it's borderline stupid, and it sucks."

"Mac, come here..."

She shook her head and stood up from her desk. "I can't. I can't kiss you right now and I certainly can't stay here tonight. I have to figure this out on my own."

"I don't see what there is to figure out," Ellington said. "I mean...are you so frightened of this that you're thinking of walking out?"

She *had* briefly considered it but to hear it from his voice was a little terrifying. It actually brought a lump to her throat and tears to her eyes—all of which she managed to push away before they got the better of her.

"No. I just...I don't know. I need to know that you'll be there. If I'm going to be this damned reliant on someone else and not let it wreck me, I have to know you'll be there. And this whole suspension thing and the allegations that caused it...they shook me."

"Of course I'll be there," he said. "Mac...what else can I do to show you that? You and I have been through a hell of a lot. I would hope I've proven myself."

She hated herself for it, but she knew she could not get much deeper into this conversation. She didn't trust herself to become fully vulnerable in front of him. Knowing that, she walked to him and gave him a brief embrace.

"Mac..."

"It's okay," she said, breaking the embrace and giving him a very casual kiss on the side of the mouth. "I need to get going back to Kingsville. I'll keep you posted."

"Just stay here tonight," he pleaded.

"I can't," she said. "I probably shouldn't have even left in the first place. I'll see you later."

Before Ellington could say anything else, she was out of the bedroom. She had a small packed bag in the trunk of her car and even though she knew she only had one more fresh change of clothes, she did not want to extend her stay by packing. Surely Kingsville had a Laundromat somewhere.

She left the apartment with only one clear certainty: that it wasn't an issue she had with Ellington at all; the problem she had was more with herself. And it had taken Ellington's suspension and the tension that came with it to point that out to her.

Whatever it was, it was still not at the top of her priority list. And maybe that was the problem. While she was still in the midst of an open case with a killer who had accumulated three bodies in the course of a week, she had no time for drama or emotion—even when it involved Ellington.

Sure, she knew it was something she needed to work on if she ever hoped to have a normal, stable relationship. But first, she had to tend to her business. First, she had to find this killer.

Of course, now that she was back to zero leads, that was looking to be harder than ever.

It made her realize something that made her heart go cold for a moment.

If she was going to catch this killer, she had to get into his head. And since he was still on the run, she was going to have to find out how he thought, how he felt.

She was going to have to explore her own fear of heights if she hoped to know the killer better.

CHAPTER TWENTY THREE

She started at the Miller Moon Bridge. As she made her way toward the gravel road, she passed a patrol car at the edge of the place where the road was no longer paved. She slowed long enough to show the policeman her badge and ID and then rolled on down the road. When she came to the old iron bridge, she left her car running, the headlights pointed toward it.

She took her small flashlight from the glove compartment and got out. She walked onto the bridge easily enough. While old, the bridge was still steady and firm, resolute beneath her feet.

When she reached the halfway point, she shined the flashlight ahead of her. The barricaded end sat down there like a mass of darkness in the night. She traced the safety rails all the way back to her and stepped closer to them, looking out from the spot where she felt certain Malory Thomas had clung for dear life about a week or so ago.

Shining the light down toward the water, Mackenzie felt the first true pang of fear. She tried to recall when she'd discovered her fear of heights. It had never been a very strong one, even after almost falling out of a tree as a kid. There was no trauma from her past, no horrific accident; she had simply always been uneasy in high places.

Unable to see the water, Mackenzie felt that fear now. Without the water in sight, the bottom could be hundreds of feet away. For all she knew, there could be an endless chasm down there. The fact that she had actually seen what was down there helped a bit—but the fact that there was only a painful death on exposed rocks from a dried up river brought the fear right back.

Would the killer have chosen this bridge if there was water down there?

The question was an intriguing one. She wondered for a moment if perhaps the height of these places wasn't affecting the killer in a fearful way. Maybe he was some sort of a thrill seeker, the type who *loved* to be in high places. But if that were true, why taint a source of enjoyment with those he planned on killing?

Maybe it's all part of the rush, she thought.

She stayed there for a few more moments, until the fear dissolved away into nothing more than a gradual unease. She went back to her car and left Miller Moon Bridge, waving at the officer at the end of the road as she passed him by.

She wondered if there would be any cars stationed out by the state-maintained road that led to the water tower. It came down to a mental game of cat and mouse, really. If there were cops patrolling the road leading to the bridge, why not the water tower? The killer would likely assume this was the case, wouldn't he? So really, it might make sense to *not* post a car by the road to the water tower. It was a crapshoot anyway, since the water tower could be accessed through the forest.

Still, as Mackenzie neared the back road that led to the land the water tower sat on, she did in fact see a patrol car. She extended the same courtesy she had at the bridge, pulling up to the car and showing her ID.

The cop in the car rolled down his window, basically asking Mackenzie to do the same.

"It's been quiet," he said. "Just one truck came through and that was two teenagers just out riding around. Probably looking for a place to make out."

"Are there any cars on the dirt road that leads to the access out in the woods?"

"No. I've kind of been swapping back and forth between the two."

"Okay. Maybe make a call to the station and let them know I'll be going in from that way."

"Will do. Everything okay?"

"Yes," Mackenzie said. "Just doing some routine check-up work."

The cop nodded, waved his thanks, and rolled the window back up. Mackenzie continued on her way, driving to the dirt road that led to the field Maureen Hanks and Bob Tully had frequented for their trysts. She parked her car at the edge of the field, retrieved her flashlight again, and went walking out into the woods.

She walked as quietly as she could, figuring that if the killer had, for some reason or another, revisited the scene of the crime by way of the forest, she would not alert him. She made her way through the trees and came out at the weeded clearing. The water tower stood in front of her and in the darkness, it seemed larger than she remembered.

She came to the ladder at the backside of the tower and looked up. With a heavy sigh, she pocketed the flashlight, still on with the bulb facing skyward, and started climbing up the ladder. She ascended with nothing more than the quiet of the night around her. The sounds of the night escorted her, tree frogs and whippoorwills singing. While these sounds were usually welcome and even pleasant to her, they seemed ominous as she made her way to the platform.

It was the final rung that made her panic a bit—the moment where she had to grab the edges of the support railings and take that one final step up onto the platform, where her foot dangled out into open air for a single moment.

When she was finally standing on the platform with both feet securely grounded, her heart settled a bit but then seemed to remember that she was still a good distance in the air. How high had Deputy Andrews told her it was?

About one hundred and thirty feet...

She took a deep breath. It was harder to handle this without someone there with her. The other night, she'd had Andrews and Tate. Before she could let the thought of Ellington assault her, Mackenzie started walking. She walked toward the front of the water tower, where Maureen Hanks had fallen from.

Her legs were surprisingly steady as she walked around to the front. She kept one hand on the smooth surface of the tower face and another on the rail to her right. Just as she started to gradually peer over the rail, a sudden motion in front of her caught her attention.

Her heart hammered in her chest and for some strange reason, she thought the motion was the water tower—she feared that somehow, she was falling.

But then a fist collided with her face and she recognized the movement as an attacker.

But why the hell are they up here? she wondered as she staggered to the left from the impact of the blow.

She felt the attacker on her, trying to pin her to the tank surface of the tower. Before he could get a firm grip on her, Mackenzie slipped quickly downward and slid around behind

him, partially tripping him as she did so. As he stumbled forward, she threw her shoulder into his back. He slammed into the tower, sending a hollow *thunk* sound out into the night as she kept her weight and momentum against his back.

Mackenzie scrambled for her handcuffs and it only took that single moment for the attacker to surprise her with a very primitive move. He lifted up his left foot and just as Mackenzie braced herself to dodge a poorly aimed kick, he instead brought it down hard on her left foot.

Taken by surprise (and fearing that at least two of her toes were bow broken), Mackenzie let her weight come momentarily free of the attacker. He took this moment to wheel around, striking her in the chest with his elbow.

She tumbled backward and when the small of her back struck the protective rail, her heart seemed like it was trying to jump right out of her chest. She used it to support herself, throwing out a kick that landed along the guy's hip.

"Who are you?" he bellowed as he staggered back.

The question itself and the way he asked it made Mackenzie aware that this was the killer. Not only was he attacking her without cause, but the manner in which he asked this question made her feel as if she had interrupted something very private. Perhaps he had come back to revisit the scene of the crime—to test his fear or to relive the death of Maureen Hanks most likely.

She didn't bother answering him. She very seriously doubted hearing that she was from the FBI would cause him to stop the attack. Already, he was coming for her again as she tried to draw in breath from his last attack. He threw a punch that she easily blocked but still, she was fighting up against the rail with nothing but open space and one hundred and thirty feet to the ground behind her.

He seemed to sense this and came surging forward with his hands open toward her. It was the first time she had seen his face clearly and she did her best to commit it to memory. He was wearing a hooded sweatshirt, the hood covering most of the top of his face, his eyes almost covered.

She acted on impulse, jabbing a hard right hand toward him. It landed squarely in his throat. He started gagging immediately but his extended arms still struck her. Mackenzie felt her back arching, her legs losing their fight with his force. As he finally backed away, she feared that it was too late. She was falling backward, starting to totter over the edge of the rail as her feet came up.

She quickly wrapped her left arm around the rail, catching it in the crook her elbow. This stopped her momentum as the upper half of her body dangled precariously over the rail, out into open space.

With her right hand, she reached for her sidearm. The attacker, still clutching his throat as he staggered back against the tower, saw this. He let out a garbled curse through his gagging and hacking and made a run for it back toward the ladder.

Mackenzie finally managed to right herself, her feet once again firmly on the platform. She drew her gun and tried to give chase but her legs were wobbly and her heart felt like it might burst. Adrenaline spiked through her, making her lightheaded as she tried to follow after him.

"FBI!" she screamed as she reached the ladder. When she looked down, she saw that the suspect was over halfway down.

She thought about taking a shot, maybe taking him in the arm, but it was too damn dark and the last thing she wanted to do was accidentally blow the guy's brains out. She'd dropped the flashlight somewhere in the skirmish and simply could not see him.

With the Glock still in her hand, she started to make her way down the ladder. She still felt disoriented from nearly having been shoved off the water tower so she had to truly focus on each rung. She was disoriented for a moment, making the act of climbing down very dangerous. She pulled herself toward the ladder, bracing herself and willing her nerves and pain to calm the fuck down.

She started down again, this time pushed by sheer determination more than anything else. When her feet touched the ground, she resented the way she had behaved for the last twenty or so seconds. Her face was aching from the punch and she was pretty sure she'd have a bruise right across her breasts tomorrow from the elbow blow. More than that, she felt like a scared little girl who had just come out of a dark room.

She strode across the field slowly with the Glock held out in front of her. She listened closely, willing the suspect to snap a twig or branch somewhere, anything to give away his location. The hell of it was that she had no idea where he had fled to. She'd been so preoccupied with not falling off of the ladder that she'd lost track of him.

She stopped moving altogether, even going so far as to hold her breath. She closed her eyes and listened as intently as she could.

Something moved far off to her right, in the opposite direction of where she had parked her car. She turned her head that way and saw nothing but the rugged tree line. Still, she ran as quietly as she could in that direction. She stopped when she reached the edge of the forest, again putting all of her focus on listening.

This time, she heard nothing.

And with every second that passed, she knew that the killer gained more and more of an advantage. Given that, she knew what she had to do. And it ate at her insides like acid.

She was going to have to call Tate and get assistance. She'd likely had the killer right in front of her, pinned to the side of the water tower, and he'd gotten away.

Swallowing down the bitterest humble pie she'd ever tasted, she pulled out her cell phone and placed the call.

CHAPTER TWENTY FOUR

Mackenzie stood her ground by the water tower until she saw the first glare of headlights coming forward, breaking through the thin grove of forest between the field where she had parked and the water tower clearing. It had taken less than three minutes after her call for the first car to arrive. When the man came through the forest, she saw without surprise that it was the officer she had passed at the entrance road. As he came tearing through the brush, more headlights came crawling toward them from behind him.

Ten minutes later, the area was abuzz with activity. Sheriff Tate and Officer Roberts stayed huddled around her while Deputy Andrews and eight other officers scoured the field for footprints or any signs of passage.

Tate in particular had wasted no time in grilling her. He wasn't meaning to be aggressive or over the top; Mackenzie knew this but was still a little put off by his in-your-face demeanor. It was a side of him she had not seen yet.

"Did you get a look at the guy?" he asked no more than ten seconds after arriving on the scene.

"Sort of. I'm guessing average height—no more than six feet tall. He was wearing a hooded sweatshirt. Black, I think. Not quite a beard on him…just a noticeable five o'clock shadow.

"Young or old?" Tate asked.

"I don't know. Older than twenty, probably no older than forty."

Tate nodded but he looked just as frustrated as Mackenzie felt. With his hands on his hips, he looked around the clearing. It was illuminated by headlights, throwing their shadows out an impossible distance until they were swallowed up by the forest.

"How much of a head start does he have on us?" Roberts asked. He seemed to be a little more clear-headed, doing his best to remain rational and logical.

"No more than five minutes passed between my call to you and the first officer getting here."

"And you have no idea which direction he headed?"

"I think he headed that way," she said, pointing slightly to the right and behind them.

"Shit," Tate said. "There's a maze of old logging roads and ATV paths back there. If he knows them well, we'll be looking forever."

"But there are no houses back there," Roberts pointed out. "He'd have nowhere to hide except in the woods."

A hundred different thoughts went racing through Mackenzie's mind. She figured that a call to the State Police could maybe get a canine unit out here by morning. But morning would be too late and by then, the killer could easily be holed up somewhere, hiding. Although Kingsville was a small backwoods town, it was also the kind of town that made it very easy to hide if you knew the layout well.

Beyond all of that, there was something else. Something about the killer. The fact that he was here and had attacked her right away—that meant something. It pulled at the edge of her deductive logic but there was no way she'd tease out the thread while standing in the headlights and chaos of the water tower clearing.

"Excuse me," she said. "I need to call this in to my director."

Tate again only gave one of his frustrated nods as he marched off to join another bunch of officers over near the edge of the trees.

Mackenzie headed back through the edging of trees, hurrying to her car. She had no idea how McGrath was going to react to this sudden turn of events—that she'd had the asshole right in her grasp and he's managed to get away. And her excuse? That she was battling with her own fear of heights at the time? That she was distracted by Ellington? That she was beginning to question her real motivations now that she had started to understand what life might be like without Ellington?

All of those were shit excuses and she knew it. So she could only call McGrath with one thing: the truth.

She placed the call, stared up into the flawless country night sky, and waited.

"Yeah?" McGrath answered.

"I'm here in Kingsville," she said, hating the way she felt. "And there have been some pretty drastic developments."

***

McGrath had handled it much better than Mackenzie had been expecting. He'd expressed concern over her injuries (which she was already beginning to feel were superficial at best) and then mentioned sending Harrison down to assist.

"I don't think that's necessary," Mackenzie said. "This is a local guy, used to the forests and the back roads. It's going to be the local guys that provide the most help, not another suit and tie from DC."

"Did you see enough of him to give the local PD anything to go on?"

"Everything I saw was generic," she said. She went through the same description she had given Tate—the five o'clock shadow, the age range, and so on.

"That really isn't much, is it?" he said. "Well, I'm sure I don't have to say this but I will anyway. If he gets that close to you again, you damn well better not let him escape again."

"Roger that," she said and killed the call.

She remained in her car, thinking back over the scene on the water tower. She played the scuffle over in her mind, looking for some detail she might have missed. The punch had caught her off guard and, if he had been punching from the other direction, that blow alone might have sent her over the edge of the platform.

But it hadn't. She had been struck from the left, which had sent her toward the tank at the top of the tower.

He hit me with his left hand, she thought. *He's a leftie.*

It was a small detail but in a town the size of Kingsville, she thought it might actually narrow down the pool of suspects substantially.

There was something else, too. That thought that had teased her out in the field moments ago. It pertained to why the killer had been there in the first place. And, she thought, it pretty much eliminated the idea that the killer was scared of heights. Even if he'd wanted to somehow recapture the murders, to relive them from the murder scenes, a legitimate fear of heights would not have made it very enjoyable.

Not only that, but he'd fought well from that height.

He isn't scared of heights. And I have no real indications that any of the victims were, either. This guy was here tonight to revel in his work, not to continue to fight off a fear. He's not afraid—and he probably never was.

In other words, she was going about this all wrong. She had been from the start, or so it seemed.

She got back out of the car and hurried back out to the clearing. She found Tate easily enough, as he was pacing back and forth between two clusters of officers that were beginning to walk into the forests, flashlights aimed into the tangle of trees ahead of them.

109

"One more detail," she said as she approached him. "This guy...he's left-handed. When he punched me, it was with his left hand."

"You positive?"

"Nearly one hundred percent."

"Any other small details coming to you?" he asked. Again, he wasn't trying to come off as a dick but apparently, that's just how he behaved when under intense pressure.

"No," she said. "But I do think I've been coming at this all wrong."

"That's bad, right?"

"No. It means now I can start from scratch. And sometimes, that's the best way to gain perspective."

She'd heard that in some class during her time at Quantico. She just hoped to hell it proved to be true in this case.

**

Three and a half hours later, a suspect had still not been found. Tate, though, seemed to hang on the left-handed detail and told her he'd let her know if anything came up. Mackenzie then took advice from both Tate and McGrath. She left the site, giving up the search, and went back to her motel room.

It was a little before one o'clock before she was showered and getting into bed. With the lights out, she feared that she might have that dream again, of falling forever off of some nameless bridge while corn husks slapped at her from all sides.

She drifted off for only a while before she stirred awake. Something had woken her up. She looked at the bedside clock and saw that it was 1:22. She hadn't been sleeping long at all. But what had woken her up?

The sound came again. A knocking at the room's door.

Tate? she wondered. *But if so, why didn't he just call like he said he would?*

She got out of bed slowly, grabbing her Glock as she did so. She slowly peered through the little glass peephole. Confused at what she saw, she opened the door immediately.

Ellington stood on the other side.

"Hey," he said sheepishly. "I heard about what happened."

She stepped aside, allowing him in. "How?"

"McGrath called. He asked if I thought you were okay to handle this on your own. Something about the suspect being in your grasp. He said there was a fight."

"There was," she said. "And yeah, he got away."

He looked at her in the light, tilting his head slightly to look at where she had been punched in the face. She knew that it had swollen a bit but the pain wasn't that bad.

"You okay?" Ellington asked.

"Yes. Well...I don't know. Aren't you going to get an ass-chewing for being here?"

"Well, I was sort of hoping you wouldn't tell anyone."

"This is dumb. You could get into a lot of trouble."

He sat on the edge of the bed as Mackenzie closed the door. "I know," he said. "But I've been thinking a lot about some of the things you said at the apartment. About how it scares you to rely on someone that you don't know for sure will always be there."

"Yeah, it's unfair for me to burden you with that and—"

"It's not a burden," Ellington said. "And I guess that's why I'm here." He reached out for her hand, which she offered without much resistance. "I heard you'd been attacked and that things were getting out of control down here and I had to be here with you. There wasn't even a question. It's why I honestly don't really care if I get my hand slapped for it. Shit...I'm already suspended. What else could happen?"

"For starters, you could lose your job."

"Doubtful. You don't think McGrath has at least some sort of an idea that I came directly to Kingsville when he told me you had been attacked? Anyway...what I'm saying is the way that relying on me scares you, the sense of protectiveness I have for you scares me, too. I've been in love before so I won't even try that line on you. But I can honestly say I've never cared so much about the well-being and safety of someone. Maybe it has to do with being partners at work. I don't know. But I heard you were in danger and my heart hurt because I couldn't be with you right then, that very second. And maybe that's why these allegations against me are wedging between us so hard. We're both scared in our own way and something like this sort of serves as bait. If we want a way out, here it is."

"And do you?" she asked.

"Hell no. If I did, I wouldn't have sped down here to see you. In fact, I'm here for something else. Look...I love that you rely on me. And I also sort of love that I'm so protective of you. So let's just gel those two together."

"How?"

He shrugged, stood up, and drew her close. "Marry me."

The words *Are you crazy?* were on her tongue, but she swallowed them back. She'd wanted some sign of consistency and safety from him and he was delivering. And while she was not quite ready to give a yes or no response to his request, the absolute sincerity in his eyes when he said those two words told her all that she needed to know.

Instead of responding with words, she responded with a kiss. Within seconds it had evolved into a melting heat, a kiss that was slow and lingering but, at the same time, communicated one thousand things to the rest of their bodies. Her jaw ached a bit from the punch she had taken as she opened her mouth to him but that ache was gone as he slowly laid her down on the bed and expertly removed her shirt.

She lost herself then, somehow allowing vulnerability. She allowed herself to fall and, for a moment, did not fear the heights she had peered down from earlier in the night. If all falling was like this, certainly there were ways to overcome such a fear.

Something about this clicked in her mind and she stored it away for a moment as she and Ellington fell into a familiar rhythm—a rhythm that even then, she knew she *could* live with for the rest of her life.

CHAPTER TWENTY FIVE

Mackenzie was about to get into the shower the next morning when her cell phone rang. It was just after six in the morning, the time of day when any call coming to an agent likely meant something big…or discouraging. Ellington, still asleep in bed, jerked awake at the sound. Still naked from the night's activities, Mackenzie grabbed her phone and saw Tate's number of the display.

"Good morning, Sheriff," she said.

"Agent White, we're pretty certain we've got a guy that fits your description. And I think you're right. I think we were all coming at it from the wrong angle right from the start."

"Who's the suspect?"

"A local guy named Jimmy Gibbons. Twenty-nine years old, a noted left-handed guy. He also has a reputation for dressing sort of grungy. Has a preference for black hooded sweatshirts."

"That all seems pretty generic."

"That's what we thought, too. But there's more. Look, come on down to the station as soon as you can. I'll bring you in on what we've got and unless you have any objection, it's looking like we might raid his home."

"Why not just pay him a friendly visit?" Mackenzie asked. She decided she'd have to skip her shower, already slipping her pants on.

"Well, there's a little more to it. Come on down and we'll fill you in."

Mackenzie ended the call and continued to get dressed. It was a little strange to be in such a better place this morning, primarily because Ellington had showed up and made the grandest of gestures.

"A break in the case?" Ellington asked, sitting up in bed.

"The local PD thinks so. I'm heading down there now to check on things."

"I'd love to ride along," he said. "But you and I both know that might not be the smartest idea. Anything I can do for you from here?"

"Yes, actually. It'll be monotonous, though."

He shrugged as he also slid out of bed and started to collect his clothes. "Might as well put me to use. I sure as hell didn't come to Kingsville for a vacation."

"Use my laptop to get into the bureau database and see if you can find any other cases in the last three years or so where suicides from jumping had some big question marks...maybe not everyone was convinced they were suicides. Don't stray too far from the Virginia, DC, Maryland area."

"Yeah, I can do that. Keep me posted on how things play out."

"I will," she said. She fixed her hair quickly, barely even glancing at it in the mirror. She then turned around and kissed Ellington, a lingering kiss that served as an aftershock of what had happened last night.

"Be careful out there," Ellington said. "And please try not to climb up on anything high again."

"I make no promises," she said with a wink as she opened the door and stepped outside.

***

Tate had assembled his small team in the conference room and they all regarded Mackenzie with enthusiasm and respect when she came into the room. The room was thick with the smell of coffee and the unmistakable feeling of excited tension among men with a similar goal in mind.

Andrews and Roberts were at the table, neither of them sitting. They both stood, looking like bulls about to be released from their gates at a rodeo.

"Just in time," Tate said. "I was about to brief Officer Roberts on what we've got. As I told you on the phone, Agent White, the suspect's name is Jimmy Gibbons. He's a twenty-nine-year-old local and we've got it confirmed that he *is* left-handed. He works at a small engine repair shop on the edge of town, one of only four employees, including the owner. Black hoodies are basically his thing—wears them constantly, even when most people have switched over to T-shirts for warmer weather."

"Again, though," Mackenzie said, "while that's a huge connection, it's also very coincidental."

"Not in Kingsville. Seems that Jimmy Gibbons hasn't reported in for work in about a week. I got that directly from his supervisor. It's also telling that Jimmy has a record. Punched his girlfriend a few years ago. No damage, but still. He did three months behind bars for it. He's also the type that seemed to spawn rumors about himself. Rumors that, in a town like this, usually tend to be true."

"What kind of rumors?" she asked.

"That Jimmy was that awkward teen that shot stray cats with a slingshot," Andrews said. "The type that set small fires just to watch bugs burn."

"And while his record only has the one incident with an ex-girlfriend," Tate said, "he's been reported twice for suspicious activity: slowly stalking across people's front yards and trespassing."

"Is that his record?" she asked, pointing to a thin folder in front of Tate.

Tate nodded and slid the folder over toward her. Mackenzie opened it up and skimmed it. She was more interested in the small photo of Jimmy Gibbons. She tilted her head and then placed her hand over the top quarter of his head. The photo only showed a very thin growth of hair on his face, so she did her best to imagine a five o'clock shadow like the one she had seen on the chin and jaws of the man from last night.

"What do you think?" Tate asked.

Mackenzie took one last look at the bottom half of the face and then tossed the folder on the table.

"I think I want to ride with you on the way to this raid."

CHAPTER TWENTY SIX

Mackenzie was coming to realize that every back road in and around Kingsville looked exactly the same; they were nothing more than long winding stretches of blacktop that meandered through the country. They were almost identical with the exception of a break in the trees for fields or smalls trips of land where houses had been thrown up. Riding in Tate's passenger seat, she almost felt like she was on some strange roller coaster taking her over dips and rises into unknown places.

Jimmy Gibbons lived down a lengthy gravel drive where a few other houses stood off of the road. The entire stretch of land looked like a trailer park, only with lower-class houses instead of mobile homes. Slanted porches, roofs in need of some work, ancient air conditioners hanging out of dingy windows, dripping pools of water onto the lawn. Tate pulled into a small dirt driveway in front of one of those houses with another car behind them, carrying Andrews and Roberts.

"His supervisor says he's tried calling three times and Jimmy never answers," Tate said. "My bet is that he's not here."

"Based on what happened to me and the circumstances you've already pointed out, we have the authority to go in anyway."

"You ever kicked a door down?" Tate asked, a bit sarcastically.

"Yes, actually. More than I care to admit."

He parked the car and they got out together. The morning was quiet with the exception of a dog barking manically somewhere further off down the long gravel road they had come down. They waited for Roberts and Andrews to join them and then approached the dingy front porch as a foursome in a single file line.

Mackenzie gestured for Tate to take the lead, wanting to give him full authority in his own backyard. He wasted no time, knocking hard on the door and instantly calling out. "Jimmy! Jimmy Gibbons! Answer the door!"

The porch was quiet. Even the barking dog off in the distance fell silent. Mackenzie had been in this same situation enough times to sense that there was no one home. Tate looked at her and she nodded.

"You have five seconds," Tate yelled, "or we're coming in regardless."

While Tate did not bother counting out loud, he did wait a full five seconds before throwing his shoulder into the door. He rebounded off if it, though it did buckle in its frame. Frustrated, he then drew his foot back and delivered a fierce kick. He staggered a bit but the door popped open, cracking the frame that held it.

As Tate collected himself, Mackenzie stepped inside. She didn't pull her Glock free, but her right hand habitually went to it and hovered there. Inside, she found a home that was not quite in a state of squalor, but one that had not seen a caring or loving touch in a very long time. The place had the smell of dust and old food. The living room, which was the first room from the front door, was furnished with an old stained rug, a recliner, a single lamp, and a television. DVDs were scattered here and there, as well as bits of newspapers and magazines.

Slowly, Tate came in behind her. Andrews and Robert followed, flanking him and then heading elsewhere into the house. Mackenzie looked around the living room for a moment but found nothing of interest—certainly nothing that would pin three murders on Gibbons.

She made her way into a small hallway off of the living room that led to one of the house's two bedrooms. Andrews was already there, gingerly leafing through a few stacks of papers that sat on an old oak desk against the far wall.

"Anything?" Mackenzie asked.

"Just some really messed up drawings. He seems to be pretty gifted artistically. Just…well, fucked up in the head."

Mackenzie looked through the stack of papers and saw what he meant. There were profiles of faces that looked to have been shot in the head, portions of the brow and forehead missing. There were graphite sketches of bodies on the ground, pools of lead around them. Mackenzie wondered if these drawings were the imagined results of people falling from high places. She scattered them out across the desk. There were eleven of them in all and she took quick snapshots of each one with her phone.

Other than the scattered papers on the desk, the room was uncluttered. The bed was made and the walls held not a single picture. A single dresser stood on the same wall as the desk. Mackenzie looked through the drawers and found only clothes (including lots of black hoodies as Tate had indicated) and, in one of the top drawers, a thumb drive.

She took the drive out and showed it to Andrews. "Any chance you think there's a laptop here?"

"Doubtful," he said. "If so, he should have sold the damn thing and got a better house. Laptop would be worth more than this dump."

Ignoring Andrews's attitude toward the place, Mackenzie pocketed the thumb drive and checked elsewhere in the house. She went into the bathroom and looked for any signs of medications. There was no medicine cabinet, just a little plastic tote shoved in the back of the small linen closet. There was nothing in it other than over-the-counter meds and Band-Aids.

Although Tate and his men seemed to conduct a thorough investigation of the house, Mackenzie followed behind them. The kitchen was sparse. There wasn't even a table in it or the very small dining area that sat adjacent to it. The fridge was stocked with beer, milk, some cheese, and a partially opened container of bologna.

In the other, smaller bedroom, she saw the only photograph in the place. It was a photo of a couple, hand in hand, walking along what appeared to be a pier. The photo was a bit older and the attire of the couple made Mackenzie assume it had been taken sometime in the early eighties.

As she was looking at it, Tate came into the room. "It's the only picture in the place," he said. "That seem weird to you?"

"Maybe a bit," she said. "Depends on his personality, I suppose. Any idea who they are?" Tate shrugged. "I've only been in town for twelve years. I'm not one of those small-town sheriffs that know the town history and everyone's family tree. If I had to put money on it, I'd assume it's Jimmy's parents."

"I'd make that same assumption," she said. "Do you know anything about them?"

He shook his head. "Nothing. I can call down to the station and get someone to look into it, though. If you think it's necessary. Maybe Andrews or Roberts will know something, too."

"Might not be a bad idea," she said. "We need to know *something* about him other than he's left-handed and hasn't shown up to work in a week."

"Did you see the drawings in the bedroom?" Tate asked.

She nodded and then showed him the thumb drive. "Found this, too. I didn't see a laptop in your car. Did I miss it?"

"No…no laptop. Just a tablet."

"I'd like to see what's on this as soon as possible," she said.

"As soon as you're done here, we can rush back to the station and get you a laptop. In the meantime, I can have someone digging up information about Jimmy's parents and as much other stuff in his past as we can get."

"I think we're good here," she said. "I get the feeling he never really spent much time at home anyway."

She wasn't sure if this was relevant to the case or not. It felt like the sort of place someone might simply check in and sleep and nothing else. She imagined Jimmy Gibbons out in the forests, perhaps studying Miller Moon Bridge and the water tower. Maybe he looked at them with the same discernment as someone who looked up to the night sky. Or maybe he looked to them as something else.

And with that thought in her mind, she looked back to the photo of the couple on the wall. It seemed eerie in the absence of anything else within the house. When she turned away to leave, she felt as if the people in that picture were watching her go, their eyes settling in on her like they were waiting to tell her something.

***

True to his word, Tate had Mackenzie behind a laptop as soon as they got back to the station ten minutes later. He set it up in his own office, closing himself and Mackenzie in the office by themselves. There seemed to be a little jealousy among Andrews and Roberts, all of which did not affect Tate at all. Mackenzie realized that the more she got to see the sheriff at work, the more she appreciated him.

She inserted the thumb drive and brought up the file directory. She felt a sickening dread in her stomach when she saw the directory. There were numerous JPEG icons; roughly one hundred of them in all. Apparently, Tate felt the same sensation at seeing the multiple rows of JPEGs.

"Shit," he said. "This is going to be bad, isn't it?"

She didn't bother trying to soften things for him. Sure, there was always the chance that the pictures might be nothing more than porn. But so far, this case suggested that something so innocent was not worth hiding. No, she expected much worse.

She clicked the first image and her hunch was proven correct.

The first image showed a figure lying face down on concrete. Blood, bits of skull and gore, and other dark material littered the ground all around the body. The left knee was bent back, the right foot shattered. While she had no way of knowing for sure, she was pretty sure this was a body that had fallen from a great height.

The second image was much of the same. This time, though, the body was lying on its side. The lower half of the face had essentially been pulverized. The victim appeared to be an Asian woman, relatively young.

"Jesus," Tate said from behind her.

Mackenzie knew what the other images held, but she had to do her job. She had to be as thorough as possible.

After several pictures, the means of death changed. The first dozen or so looked to be suicides via jumping. She ruled out the idea that they were all Jimmy Gibbons's victims within five pictures. The backgrounds of a few of them showed entirely different cities. One was somewhere in Japan while another looked to be somewhere in New York if the signage in the background was any indication.

Following the supposed jumpers, she saw images of other suicides. Gun blasts to the head, some with powerful guns. Slit wrists in a bathtub. She saw one where it looked like a man had tried to decapitate himself with a skill saw.

"This guy's a sicko," Tate said. "How in the hell did he get these pictures anyway?"

"You'd be surprised how easy it is to get this sort of thing online," Mackenzie said. "A few of them are pretty clearly photos taken from crime scenes—probably even somehow taken from case files."

"But why?" Tate asked. He was no longer even looking at the pictures. Instead, he was facing the door, as if anxious to be away from the laptop.

"Could be any number of reasons," she said. "But based on these pictures, I think I do get a better idea of what kind of person we're dealing with. And honestly, I don't even know if any type of fear or appreciation of heights has anything to do with it. I think it's about control and some sick fascination with the destruction of his victims. He's trying to make as big of a mess as he can."

"So what the hell do we take away from this?" he asked.

It was a good question, one that she was focused on enough to close out of the visceral and morbid pictures. "For some reason, it's about gore for him," she said. "Shock value. All of those pictures...the bodies were in terrible shape. I feel like most of them were either suicides or intentional violent crimes. But there was not one single picture of someone hanging from a noose, or slumped over dead in their car from suffocating on the exhaust fumes."

"So he's not only killing these people, he's trying to make a mess out of doing it," Tate said.

"Yeah, it seems that way."

"So how the hell are we supposed to know who the next victim is?" Tate asked. "Or where he's going to strike next?"

Before Mackenzie could answer, there was a knock at the door. Andrews opened it and peeked his head inside. "So, we got results on Jimmy Gibbons's parents. And they're pretty damned interesting."

"Spill it, then," Tate said. "Don't tease it! We don't have time for that shit!"

"Brian and Beth Gibbons—both died in a tragic car accident. They were crossing a small country bridge somewhere in the southern part of the state. There were icy conditions and they went skidding. The barrier along the side of the bridge was old and dilapidated and the car went right over. They fell seventy feet, straight into the water. The mom died in the water and the husband died in the back of an ambulance."

"So where the hell was Jimmy Gibbons when all of this happened?"

"In the back seat. He was three at the time, in a car seat. The way the reports read, his mother died because she saved him. The father got himself and his both to safety. Jimmy was touch and go for a minute with a lot of water in his lungs but he pulled through."

"So you're telling me," Mackenzie said, "that we've got a killer throwing people from great heights that also had parents die from their own fall from a great height?"

"Looks that way," Andrews said.

Mackenzie thought hard and no matter which direction her mind tried to go, the simplest solution seemed the most logical.

"Sheriff, I realize you've got a small force here, but I think we need to stake out anything taller than fifty feet in this town."

"Well, that won't be much. There's the old Weldon Drugstore building and Glory Baptist Church. That bell tower is damn near seventy-five feet in the air, I'd guess. And there's a bunch of old grain silos, but they're all out of commission and I don't even think you can get to the tops of them anymore."

"Start with the drug store and the church," she said. "If you need to get the State guys on it, call them up."

"You think he's going to do it again?" Tate asked.

"I do," she said, pulling the thumb drive from the laptop, the images still swimming in her mind. "And I think he's going to do it sooner rather than later."

CHAPTER TWENTY SEVEN

While Tate was busy scrambling his small forces, Mackenzie sped back to the motel to meet with Ellington. When she entered the room, she found him diligently sitting behind the laptop, looking through the FBI database just like she had asked him. He looked tired and frustrated, telling her without a word how the search was going.

"Nothing, I take it?" she asked.

"There's plenty, actually," he said. "But filtering through it all would take a team. And it would be a long, grueling process. How about you? Any movement?"

"It looks like we have a very solid lead," she said. "Now it's just a matter of finding him because he seems to have split his home within the last few days."

"Any likely spots for his next victim?" Ellington asked.

"Just a few," she said. "We're looking into those right now."

"Anything I can do except sit here behind a computer?"

"No. I can't have you get into more trouble. Even if McGrath *does* know you would have come here, you have to play it smart. This harassment thing will blow over soon enough but you going in direct defiance of a suspension won't go away so easily."

"I know," he said with a sigh.

"Look...I'll send you over some pictures I took from the suspect's house. Analyze them. Scrutinize the hell out of them. Let me know if you find something—*anything*—that might tip us off about any patterns or motive she might have. I haven't had a chance to study them yet."

"Okay, I can do that. But look...I don't know if it's worth me hanging around much longer. I came last night out of protective instincts. And since you *still* haven't answered the question I asked you last night..."

"I didn't, did I?" she said playfully.

"No, you did not."

She simply nodded, kissed him on the side of the mouth, and headed for the door. "I'll send you those pictures within the next fifteen minutes or so."

As she made her way out the door, he called out to her. She wasn't sure she had ever heard him say her name with so much concern in his voice. "Mackenzie?"

"Yes?"

"Be careful out there."

"I will," she said.

They shared a heartfelt glance as she walked outside, leaving him alone with the laptop again. Knowing he was there but could not be by her side as she headed out to hopefully tie this case up made her feel impossibly lonely. And of course, his question from last night still weighed heavy on her heart.

Marriage, she thought as she raced to her car. *That came out of nowhere, didn't it?*

It had. It was an unexpected surprise, but one that had her soaring on the inside. She was pretty certain she would say yes, but she could not have that significant life event altering her mental state while she seemed to finally be getting closer to the bottom of this case.

So let's go ahead and wrap the damn thing up, she thought as she got into her car and started the engine. She called Tate and as the phone started to ring, she could feel things moving forward—the ringing of the phone almost like a signal to start a countdown. She had felt this before and it usually proved to be right. With just about any case, there came a point where she could feel the end coming—for better or for worse. She felt it now, even as Tate's voicemail picked up after just the second ring.

You really need to upgrade that fucking phone, Mackenzie thought.

She tossed the phone down. No sooner had it hit her passenger seat than it started to ring. She saw Tate's number, calling her back. A little miffed, she answered the call.

"Got an update for me?" Mackenzie asked.

"Sorry I missed your call. This damned phone…" He stopped and sighed before continuing. "We've already got three men out by Weldon's canvassing the place," Tate told her through the cell phone. "I'm headed out to Glory Baptist Church with Officer Roberts right now if you want to join us."

She agreed and listened to her phone ding twenty seconds later as Tate sent her directions. She pulled them up and for what felt like the hundredth time, found herself speeding through the twists and turns of a series of back roads that felt as if they had been totally forgotten by the rest of the world.

When she pulled her car into the square gravel parking lot on the western side of Glory Baptist Church, Tate and Roberts were already there. They were walking toward the front entrance, a rustic white door that was in terrible need of a coat of paint. The small letter board sitting in the front lawn proclaimed: SUNDAY SERVICE: 10 AM.

The church was located along one of the back roads, about a mile and a half away from what was considered the "center" of town. Like just about everything else in Kingsville, it was surrounded by open air and trees—which made the cemetery off to the back of the property seem creepy as hell. The very high bell tower was almost comically tall. Whoever had come up with the design for it when they were building the church had maybe done it as some kind of joke. Maybe a big ironic middle finger to those who would someday attend the church.

"Has anyone called the pastor?" Mackenzie asked.

"I tried," Tate said. "He's doing hospital visitation in Arlington. But his wife has been gracious enough to tell us where the spare key is."

As he said that, Tate walked up the steps and stood on this tiptoes. He leaned forward, ran his hand above the door, and found a small, loose piece of the wooden siding that made up the church's exterior. He plucked the wood free and showed them the spare key that hung by a nail on the back side of the wood fragment. He removed the key, placed the wood down on the stoop, and slid the key into the old brass lock on the door.

When they stepped inside the church, Mackenzie instantly thought of her childhood. It smelled like her grandmother's attic, where she had once sat in an old musty chair and read volume after volume of the original Nancy Drew books. Underneath that smell there was also something like lemon—muted furniture polish that had likely been swept across the back of the pews recently.

It was a small church from the inside. She looked up at the ceiling as they entered the sanctuary. It was about fifteen feet high and she tried her best to imagine the large bell tower over their heads. The three of them made their way through the sanctuary, toward the back of the room where a large door led to the rest of the building.

They then entered a large room that was occupied with a few round tables and chairs, perhaps some kind of large classroom. The attic smell wasn't as intense here, as it was drowned out by someone having mopped the floors recently. Mackenzie looked down at the floor for any clear signs that someone had recently walked through here but saw none.

The rest of the church was what Mackenzie had always assumed a small-town church would be like. A single long hallway that contained a few classrooms. A small kitchen area sat to the back of the hallway and directly in the center, a single door was closed. A small sign had been printed out in plain Times New Roman type: **Bell Tower Entrance Only!**

"Have you ever been up there?" Mackenzie asked Tate and Roberts.

"Not once," Tate said.

"This is actually the first time I've ever stepped foot in this building," Roberts said.

"We're all new here," Tate said with a nervous grin. "So you might as well lead the way."

Mackenzie opened the door and stepped inside. There was a very small alcove of sorts, a quick turn to the right, and then a set of stairs that led up at an almost dizzying angle. The stairs were made of wood and easily at least fifty years old—probably closer to one hundred. Each one creaked under her weight, echoing as Tate and Roberts followed up behind her.

She felt no immediate threat but still kept her hand close to her Glock. The closer to the top of the stairs she got, the dustier things started to get. There was very little light, coming from somewhere overhead and barely illuminating the stairwell. Just when she started to feel a little claustrophobic, she came to the top of the stairs.

There was a small landing and then a set of five more steps that led directly up into the bell tower. From where she stood, Mackenzie could look directly up into the tower, peering into the underside of the huge brass bell. She made her way up the other small set of stairs and stood within the tower. The stairs led to a small walkway that led around the bell. She made her way over to the side of the tower that looked out onto the side yard of the church.

"You good up there?" Tate called from the landing below.

"Yeah. It's crowded up here, though. Hang tight, would you?"

Tate seemed fine with that as Mackenzie walked along the circumference of the tower. The bell itself was quite fascinating, a beautiful shade of brass that had only been made even more stunning by its exposure to the elements through the square window-like openings along the side of the tower.

She looked out of the three openings, trying to recapture that sense of being above it all that she had felt on Miller Moon Bridge and on the walkway of the water tower. It took her a moment to realize that she was not going to find it here. The space was too enclosed. More than that, the drop was not a drop straight down. If someone fell out of one of the openings along the sides of the bell tower, they'd strike the roof first, hitting about twenty-five feet down.

There was simply no sense of freedom up here, no sense of being in control. If anything, the presence of the bell made it extremely crowded. While forcing someone up those stairs might be easy enough, pushing them forcibly along the walkway around the bell would be a painstaking process. Not to mention, they'd have to break in just to gain access to the tower in the first place.

She headed back for the stairs, shaking her head. "No dice," she said as she walked back down to the landing where Tate and Roberts waited for her. "It's just too crowded. And the drop is interrupted by the roof. If our killer is getting his thrills by dropping people from heights to watch them hit the ground below, this isn't the place."

"You want to head over to Weldon's Drug and get a feel for it?" Tate asked.

"Might as well," she said. But even then, she felt like it would be a dead end, too. Something about the idea of the killer operating from a confined space—even an abandoned building with a series of large and easily accessible windows—didn't seem to line up with what she had seen of his work so far. Still, she wanted to remain thorough and if that meant visiting a potential murder site that she was pretty sure would not pan out, so be it.

Besides, the alternative was reporting back to McGrath, letting him know that she was still coming up empty on this case. Given that, she marched back down the bell tower stairs with Tate and Roberts ahead of her. She still felt the sensation of the case coming to an end but started to wonder if it was going to be a *successful* end.

CHAPTER TWENTY EIGHT

He felt entirely exposed, walking across the lawn in the sunlight. He'd been hiding in the forest and even under the porches of unsuspecting people for the last week or so. To be back out in the light made him feel like he was risking his life. It made him feel like a vampire, which was fine with him. Maybe it wouldn't be so bad to be a vampire. Because whatever he was...he felt it was much, much worse than the blood-sucking undead.

As he had slunk along the edges of the forest in preparation of getting his next victim, he had seen the cop cars whizzing by. He'd never seen such activity out of the police before, not during the ten years he'd lived in this awful little town. They were up to something—probably trying to find him or to figure out why he was doing the things he was doing.

Good luck with that, he thought with a little smile.

He looked at the house ahead of him. It was a nice house, one that he might have lived in at some point if his parents had not died when he'd been a young boy. He knew his parents had decent jobs when they had died and figured he might have eventually had a good life. He'd be popular in high school, go to college, get a good job, get married, have a few kids.

But he'd ended up with none of that. His parents had died and all of those dreams he'd had of a life imagined had died with them, falling helplessly into a river that had taken both of their lives.

He walked across the yard and up onto the porch of the idyllic little country house. He did his best to seem normal, as if he belonged there. He had changed out of his black hoodie, opting for just a plain white T-shirt. He figured after the run-in with the cop on the water tower last night, they'd be looking for someone wearing a black hoodie. He felt naked without it, even more exposed.

He pushed that feeling to the back of his head as he came to the front door of the house. He knocked lightly, casually, and did his best to put on a smile even though his insides felt like they were on fire. He'd been living on a pure adrenaline rush ever since he'd demanded that Malory Thomas strip naked in front of him while holding the gun to her head. That adrenaline had not evaporated when he had tried to do things to her but had ultimately failed.

Apparently, too much adrenaline and nerves made it hard to get sexually excited—something he had been very sad to realize.

It had also not evaporated when he'd watched her slam into the rocks beneath Miller Moon Bridge. Sadly, *that's* what had gotten him excited, the parts of him that had failed him while she had stripped standing at full attention as he stared at her broken body beneath the bridge.

He saw that moment in his memory as if it were just some long-ago movie he had seen. Right now, he was more focused on the door in front of him. He knocked once more, keeping that forced smile on his face.

Finally, someone answered the door. The woman saw him, gave a very brief frown, and then tried on a smile of her own.

"Jimmy," she said. "What are you doing here?"

"Sorry," he said. "I know I don't have an appointment. But I really need to talk to you."

Dr. Jan Haggerty nodded and sighed. "Well, come on in. I'm with a client right now but I can see you for a bit when I'm done. You can sit in the den while I finish up."

"Thanks, Dr. Haggerty," Jimmy said.

He followed her in and when they split ways while she returned to her office and Jimmy went into her den, he dropped the fake smile.

It was hard to smile when he was this scared.

He once again found himself wishing he was a vampire. Then he could just stay in the darkness. He did all of his work by night anyway and he apparently loved the sight of blood—something he was only now beginning to accept and understand.

If he was a vampire, maybe he wouldn't be this scared.

Or maybe not. No matter what you were, Jimmy figured, it was probably always a little spooky to realize that you were going to kill again.

That you *had* to kill again just so life might start to make some sense.

***

Jimmy Gibbons had spent time in Dr. Haggerty's den a few times before. If one of her sessions with a client ran over, her den was where the next client would sit and wait for their turn. Dr. Haggerty always kept music on in the den, played through a Bluetooth speaker, usually tuned to some new age bullshit with wind noises and minimalist piano.

Jimmy was looking through one of the books he had pulled off of her shelf—a picture book of Iceland and its fjords and skylights—when Dr. Jan Haggerty same into the den. She looked happy to see him as always. Jimmy was mostly happy to see her, too. She always made him feel welcome and warm. And even though she was a little north of fifty, Jimmy thought she was pretty hot.

"So, Jimmy," she said. "I've never known you to come by unannounced. Is everything okay?" she asked.

He shook his head. "No," he said. "I've been having nightmares about my parents again."

"Oh no," she said. "It's been a while since you've been bothered by those, hasn't it?"

"A little over a year," he said.

"Have you been drinking?" Dr. Haggerty asked.

Jimmy didn't answer right away. She was not budging from her place by the den entrance. It was quite clear that she had no intention of turning this into an actual session. And that was fine with Jimmy. Actually, he preferred it. It would make the whole messy ordeal that much easier.

"No, I haven't been drinking," he said. "But things are getting worse. I started something new…some new way to overcome it all."

"Overcome what, exactly?" Haggerty asked.

"The nightmares. The guilt. All of it."

"What have you been trying, Jimmy? Please don't tell me you're doing some sort of drug."

"Oh, I thought about it. But no…just the Xanax you prescribed for me. This other thing…I think it might be helping but it's also making me realize something else."

Dr. Haggerty finally moved away from the entranceway to the den and took a seat on the other end of the couch. "What are you doing?" she asked with an edge of worry to her voice.

"I thought maybe I could overcome it all by going up on high places. I've never been scared of heights, not really, but I avoided them. Knowing my parents went off a bridge, it seemed like tempting fate to do anything involving heights, you know? So I tried it and it didn't work at first."

"At first?"

"Yeah, there was this loneliness. I started out on Miller Moon Bridge. I went at night and just looked down to where the water should be. On moonless nights, it's like looking straight down into a pit. You can't even see where the fall ends, you know? It made me feel small, which I didn't like. But still…I think it *did* help me to put a stop to the dreams for a while. But then they started coming back and I had to try something different. I took someone up with me, Dr. Haggerty."

He stopped here and looked directly at her. He knew that the news of what he had been doing was spreading all around town. He knew that Dr. Haggerty would know all about Malory Thomas, Kenny Skinner, and Maureen Hanks. He was curious to see how she would react. He'd just given her enough to be considered a subtle confession.

"A friend of yours?" she asked.

"No. Just someone I've always sort of respected and *wanted* to get to know." He chuckled here and shook his head. "I don't think she liked it very much."

He could tell that Dr. Haggerty was doing her very best to keep her calm but her true feelings were lurking in her eyes and at the corners of her tightly drawn mouth. She was scared. She was worried.

"Jimmy, I think we need to talk at length about this as soon as possible," she said. "Let me check my calendar. I might be able to get you in tomorrow. Would that work for you?"

"Yes. Thanks. Sorry to just drop by but…I don't know. Something is happening to me and I don't know how to stop it."

Not that I want it to stop, he thought.

He waited for her to leave before he got up from the couch. He knew exactly what she was doing, and it certainly wasn't checking her calendar. He'd seen the worry on her face and he had also seen all of those police cars darting up and down the road.

He quietly followed her footsteps, leaving the den and crossing the large hallway that led into her study. She was stepping behind her desk and reaching for her cell phone. When he entered the room, she looked up and saw him. Her hand froze just above the phone.

"I've seen you book appointments for me for two years now," he said. "You don't keep your calendar on your phone."

She nodded and picked it up. "Jimmy…what have you been doing? Do you…do you need some help?"

"I think it might be too late for that," he said. "But in your own way, you *can* help me. I need you to put the phone down. Who are you going to call anyway?"

"Jimmy, this is serious," she said, sounding as if she was on the verge of tears. "There's a lady in town from the FBI. If we get you to them now, they can help."

"Maybe I don't want help," he said. "For the first time since I can remember, I feel happy. I don't know why…but something about it helps. It eases the tension. It makes the nightmares go away."

"Let me call the police," she said. "I think it's safest for everyone."

"No," he said. He started slowly walking across the room. "I need you to come with me. Maybe when we're up there, you'll understand. Maybe then you can help me…if there *is* any help. Because honestly…when they fall and they scream…it's magic. It's like a drug. I don't understand it. Maybe you could."

"Jimmy," she said, raising the phone to start dialing. "Don't do this."

"No…*you* don't do *that*," he said. And with that, he pulled the .09 millimeter from the holster hidden at the back waist of his pants.

"I *will* shoot you," he said. "I thought it was just watching people break when they fall from the bridge or the water tower. But I think it's just the mess in general. I'll be just as happy smearing your brains all over the wall. So please…put the fucking phone down."

She shuddered and did what he said. She was crying, though trying to hold most of it back. She was unlike the others. The others had wept openly, begging for their lives. Maureen had offered sex. Sex of any kind he wanted. He'd thought about it but in the end decided against it.

Maybe she *could* help him after all.

"What do you want?" she asked.

"Right now, just you. Lock your doors, forget about answering your phone or your emails. You and I are going to talk for a while before we head out. Maybe you can help me figure out why I've become this…this *monster*."

"Jimmy, you aren't a monster."

He laughed at this, his grip on the gun growing tighter.

"I don't know about that. I get harder than I've ever been when I push them. And when they hit…that sound. The cracking. The breaking. I love it. With Kenny Skinner, he hit the rocks below the bridge in a way that made his head crack open. You want to know what it sounded like?"

Dr. Haggerty shook her head.

"Have a seat," Jimmy said, pointing the gun to the couch he had sat on several times in the last few months. "I think you and I are going to have a long day together."

CHAPTER TWENTY NINE

Weldon's Drugstore had turned out to be just as big of a waste of time as Glory Baptist Church. While there was a decent drop from the back of the building to the pavement below, there were too many obstacles. To get to the third floor, a killer would have to break down a locked door to the second floor—a lock which Mackenzie had been forced to pick and had barely been able to get into at all.

Not only that, but when they had gotten to the third floor, the windows were boarded up and reinforced with some sort of wired screen.

When they left and headed back to the station, Mackenzie did not feel like she was having to resort to going back to square one. She did her best to see it as having eliminated two potential sites. On the way back to the station, Tate had called her to let her know that he had added the church and the drugstore to the rotation of the afternoon and that night's rounds for officers out on patrol.

As for Mackenzie, she knew she had to set a plan in place. Even if it meant coordinating with Tate and his men to canvass the streets all night, she had to do *something*. As she headed back to the motel, she wondered for perhaps the first time if the killer might eventually venture away from dropping his victims from tall places. In a place like Kingsville, he'd run out of options soon enough. She wondered if this case would be any easier to figure out if she could remove the bridge and the water tower from the equation. If heights were taken out, what kind of killer would he look like?

He likes to exploit his victims in some strange way, she thought. *If those pictures on the USB and his drawings are any indication, he has an enormous bloodlust. But he's patient—patient enough to make someone climb the ladder at the water tower, patient enough to capture Malory Thomas and carry her out to Miller Moon Bridge.*

She dwelled on these thoughts as she pulled her car into the motel parking lot. As much as Ellington was not going to want to take an even more distant back seat on this, she planned to take over the laptop. She actually hoped that with him there and their ability to rekindle the chemistry of their working relationship, she'd be more productive. She figured she could start by looking into any brutal murders within a fifty-mile radius over the course of the last three years or so. She could probably get Tate to look into his own files at the station to expedite the process.

However, when she entered the motel room, all of those plans and ideas froze up for a moment. Even before she had the door fully open, she heard Ellington's voice. He was speaking to someone in a pleading manner, something she was not at all accustomed to.

"...and I've done nothing at all that would be considered defiant towards a supervisor."

Mackenzie quietly closed the door behind her and stood there, giving him an inquisitive look. He shook his head slowly. She did not like the fact that he looked very worried. He then mouthed one word to her that explained everything.

"McGrath."

Her nerves instantly started to act up. She had learned how to deal with McGrath in her own way, no longer fearing the man whenever she was called to his office. But she also knew him well enough to know that while he did not use his power as an intimidation tool very often, he had no problem using it when he had no choice. By the look on Ellington's face, she wondered if that was what was going on right now.

She wanted to ask him to put the call on speaker mode but she knew all too well that McGrath would be able to tell. So she stood very close to Ellington, trying to eavesdrop. She could hear most of the words. She gathered that McGrath had somehow figured out that Ellington had not only come to see her, but that he had taken on a part in the investigation. Just as she felt she was caught up, she heard McGrath ask: *"And do you even know where in the hell White is?"*

"She actually just stepped in, sir."

Mackenzie heard McGrath tell Ellington to put her on the phone. Ellington handed it over with a sorrowful look on his face.

"This is Mackenzie," she said.

"Dammit, White...what in the hell do you think you're doing?"

"Trying to find a killer, sir."

"Don't be a smart ass. When Ellington showed up there last night, why did you not send him back home? You knew he was suspended and that having him around while you were working on an active case—an active case that seems to be going nowhere, I might add—would only make things worse for him."

"Because he and I know where to draw the line, sir," she said. "Agent Ellington would never do anything to jeopardize a case or his career."

"Bullshit. If that's the case, why do I have it on the records right here in front of me that he logged into the database two different times today, spending a total of three hours looking at files?"

Shit, she thought. *I should have thought to make sure he logged in under my account.*

"I don't know what to say, sir. I can assure you, though, that he—"

"I don't want your assurances. Where are you on this case, anyway? I assume it can't be too good if you have Ellington digging for straws while you're getting nowhere."

"It's more of the same," she said, hating to admit it. "We have a suspect that looked to be the guy but no one has seen him for nearly a week."

"Is it the guy that attacked you last night?" McGrath asked.

"It seems that way. His name is Jimmy Gibbons and he's—"

"I don't care who he is. Listen, White…Director Wilmoth has seen enough to think his nephew was indeed murdered. And he thanks you for opening that up. But he also agrees with me that this is not something you need to be wasting your time on. Between the State Police and a different pair of agents, this case can be wrapped. Given the situation with Ellington, I want both of you back here this afternoon."

"No way," she said, unable to stop the words from coming out of her mouth. "With all due respect, this town is a shithole. We'll find him soon. A day. Two at most."

"Good. Then I can send Yardley and Harrison to take care of it with the utmost confidence. I want you back here, in my office, in no more than three hours. Am I understood?"

Mackenzie gripped the phone tightly, wanting to throw it, wanting to scream at McGrath. But she buried all of that in the pit of her stomach and gritted her teeth.

"Yes sir," she hissed.

And for perhaps the first time in her FBI career, she killed the call before McGrath did.

Ellington, who had been standing directly beside her to listen in the entire time, hung his head. "I'm sorry," he said.

"Don't even try that," Mackenzie said. "This is *not* your fault."

"Well, me coming down here didn't *help* matters at all, now did it?"

"I won't argue with that," she said with just a bit of bitterness. "But I'm glad you did, which proves that maybe I'm *not* the best agent to be on this right now."

"So you're giving up just like that?"

"Yes. It's bad enough that *one* of us is suspended. I'm not trying to test McGrath's patience right now. Besides...I was able to prove that these deaths weren't suicides. With what we have and the help of Sheriff Tate and his men, I think Harrison and Yardley will be a great team to wrap this up."

"And you're fine with McGrath's decision?" he asked, perplexed.

"Hell no I'm not fine with it," she said. "But it's not worth arguing. Now can we *please* start winding things down here before McGrath decides to make your suspension permanent?"

"I guess," Ellington said. It was clear that he was not happy with the turn of events.

Mackenzie wasn't either; actually, she was pretty much furious. But she also knew that there was nothing she could do but obey McGrath's orders. Right now, one of the most important things in her life was making sure Ellington could eventually reclaim his rightful place within the bureau. And if her handing a case off to two other agents was a sign that she could play ball and might make things easier for Ellington, she was fine with it.

"Hey," she said, taking his hand. "It will be okay."

She kissed him and he nodded. "Maybe," he said. "Eventually. I think it might be better right now if you could just give me an answer to that question I asked you last night."

She smiled and said, "I'm sure it would. But for right now, I need to go let Tate know that he's going to have two other agents to babysit tomorrow."

She kissed him again and left the room. She was halfway across the parking lot toward her car when she realized that she was, in fact, so pissed off at McGrath's decision that she had made fists, digging her nails into the meat of her palms until they had made little red puncture marks, showing just the slightest bit of blood.

CHAPTER THIRTY

It all nearly seemed formulaic as far as Mackenzie was concerned. She'd met with McGrath for no more than five minutes. She gave him all of her reports, which he would turn over to Harrison and Yardley. He scolded her a bit for so willingly taking Ellington in and then thanked her for her hard work and getting Director Wilmoth off of his ass. After that, he'd sent her on her way.

She nearly went looking for Harrison, wishing him luck and filling him in, but she decided not to. She wanted him to take the case and run with it as if it were his own. If she walked into his office and went over everything with him, it would feel like she was handing him her leftovers. She knew Harrison needed to grow in his role, so she left it alone. She headed back to the apartment that she and Ellington had been sharing for the last month and a half and found him starting dinner in the kitchen.

"How's McGrath?" Ellington asked.

"Fine. He's just glad to have Wilmoth off of his case. How are *you*?"

"Decent. I got a call from the bureau attorney on the drive back from Kingsville. The woman who made the allegations is starting to have second thoughts. Apparently someone at the field office where she's working now asked her for more details before she took it all the way to court. It looks like certain details she's alleged aren't lining up."

"So you're in the clear?" Mackenzie asked.

"No. Not yet. But things are looking much better than they were yesterday."

She stepped in to help him with dinner, slicing an onion for the homemade stir fry he was making. "I'm sorry for getting so bent out of shape over your suspension," she said. "If I'm being honest, I think it just boils down to feeling betrayed—which is stupid because I didn't even know you when these things happened."

"It's okay," he said. "If the roles were reversed, I would have been jealous as hell. I get it. I think with me, though, it's just the sad fact that this is what the world has become. Men can't keep their hands to themselves so now whenever there's even a suggestion that a man has been handsy or inappropriate it *has* to be taken *this* seriously. So yeah…I think you had every right to get upset."

"I do trust you, you know."

"I know," he said, stirring the contents of the frying pan.

"And it's because I trust you that I'm even considering the question you asked me last night."

He chuckled. "I figured you wouldn't give me an outright yes or no right at the time of the proposal. It's not like you."

"The fact that you understand that and appreciate it speaks volumes," she said with a chuckle of her own.

It felt off to be doing something as domesticated as preparing a meal together when, just five hours ago, she had been exploring a little Baptist church for any signs that it might be the next scene along a murderer's path. She knew she would not be able to stop thinking about the case until the killer was captured and, as such, she found herself wanting to reach out to Harrison just to make sure he and Yardley had everything they needed. She respected Harrison a great deal and felt that with the right tutelage, he could be an amazing agent. She saw no sense in being bitter about him stepping in to finish the assignment and wished him the best.

Besides…the sooner he and Yardley brought the killer to justice, the sooner she could put it out of her mind.

She and Ellington finished out the afternoon in the way she assumed most married couples without children would. They watched the news, caught up on straightening up the apartment, and had a spontaneous quickie in the bathroom just before Ellington got into the shower.

While he showered, Mackenzie gave in to her thoughts on the Kingsville case. She texted Harrison just to get an update. She assumed that she and Yardley would be in Kingsville by now, introducing themselves to Sheriff Tate. The text she got in response a few minutes later was not at all what she had been expecting.

Nothing yet, Harrison replied. **We're heading out in the morning. Due to meet with the Sheriff around 8 am.**

Mackenzie sighed and set her phone down. The lack of urgency on McGrath's part told her all she needed to know. Whether because of a lack of results or from instruction coming from Director Wilmoth, the Kingsville case was slowly taking a back seat. She figured that unless the killer was apprehended or more bodies started piling up, it would soon be nothing more than a footnote for some agent riding a cubicle for most of the day.

She felt that this was a mistake. While McGrath had asked for her thoughts and theories about the case after pulling her off of it, he hadn't seemed too invested. She felt certain the killer would strike again and given the schedule so far, it could be any day now. Maybe as soon as tonight. The fact that there was no agency presence or even cooperation from the State Police seemed sloppy and irresponsible.

Following Harrison's response, Mackenzie knew that any hope of sleeping well that night was out of the question. She went to her laptop and looked at all of the case files she had accumulated. She didn't think McGrath would have an alert programmed for when she logged into the database but didn't want to run the risk.

When Ellington was out of the shower, she was behind the laptop, scrolling through her notes and the grisly pictures from the Kingsville PD.

"Should you be doing that?" he asked playfully.

"Someone needs to," she said. "McGrath is waiting until tomorrow to send Harrison and Yardley to Kingsville. Every murder has been after sundown. And based on the schedule this guy is keeping so far, he could hit again any night now."

"You think McGrath would hear you out?"

"Maybe," she said. "But I'd rather not take the chance. I could call him with my concerns and he might tell me to keep away from the case. Yes, he pulled me from it but he didn't tell me to drop it completely. If I can find something here to help them—or even something to send to Tate—I might be able to sleep tonight."

"Seems risky," he said. "Makes no sense for *both* of us to be suspended."

"I don't think he'd suspend me over something like this," she countered.

It was clear that Ellington wanted to push the matter, but he remained silent. He'd seen her push slightly beyond the limits of what was expected of her before. She supposed he also knew that ever since the beginning, McGrath had come to almost expect some pushback whenever he gave her orders.

And besides…whenever she had pushed back in the past, it had netted significant results. So she continued to pore over the files, taking extra care to study the small bit of information from the Kingsville PD on Jimmy Gibbons.

After a while, Ellington went into the living room and she heard the muffled sound of the television through the walls. She looked at the clock and saw that it had somehow come to be 8:45. She was starting to become convinced that she'd simply lost her opportunity to contribute to this case.

She closed down the laptop and sat at her desk, thinking. She closed her eyes and thought of the bridge and the water tower, what it had felt like to stand at the top of both of the structures while looking down at the world. Maybe it had been more than just the feeling of control for the killer—for Jimmy Gibbons.

But what else could it have been?

She thought back to her brief trip through his home, seeing that single picture of his parents on the wall. There had been something creepy about it, almost like it was a monument of some kind.

But that hadn't been the only picture in the house, had it? No, there had been the sketches Gibbons had made and the USB.

Thinking of the sketches, Mackenzie pulled them up on her phone. She scrolled through each one, both impressed and disgusted at the talent Gibbons showed with a pencil. The sketches were more than just comic book violence and gore. They were realistic, the creation of someone who had obsessed over the gruesome pictures she had found on that USB. In one of them, she even saw a very faint sketch of a bridge in the background and—

She zoomed in on the bridge. It had been drawn faintly, as if it were way off in the background. And it wasn't just any bridge. The shape of it was very familiar to her, as she had seen it several times in the last few days.

It was Miller Moon Bridge.

Slowly, see scanned through the rest of the pictures, looking for other drawings of the bridge. After four more pictures, she did not find a representation of the bridge but she *did* see something else in the background of another one. Like the sketch of the bridge, it was faint, pushed back into the distance by a light shading technique where the solid lines were barely even there at all. In this picture, the shape in the background was very easily identified as a water tower.

Daring to hope that there might be something else to find in the other sketches, Mackenzie scrolled to the next one. And right there in the next one in line, she saw what she was looking for.

"Holy shit," she whispered.

The sketched showed a body that looked as if it had been mutilated with a sledgehammer. The pools of blood looked eerily real, even done in pencil. Behind the body was what looked, at first, like scraggly lines of graphite. But then she saw the shape standing off to the right side, again shaded to appear as if it was way off in the back.

It was another shape that resembled a water tower but was distinctly different.

139

It was a grain silo, standing among those graphite smudges which Mackenzie now understood was a grain field.

That's his next stop, she thought.

She quickly looked through the other sketches for other landmarks but found none. She wasn't sure if she was looking at a sketched out set of plans or just the drawn fantasies of a killer, but instinct told her that if two of the murder sites were present in these drawings, then the image of grain silos surely meant that he would strike there, too.

She recalled Tate mentioning the silos as potential high points in Kingsville but then ruling them out because getting up to the top would be next to impossible.

She shut the picture down and pulled up Tate's number. The phone rang twice and went to voicemail just like before. Assuming he'd call her back like before, she waited a few seconds. And then she waited some more.

Apparently, Tate was going to play by the rules, not wanting to rub McGrath the wrong way. He was not going to return her call.

But then her phone rang. "This is Agent White," she answered.

"Hey, Agent White," Tate said. "What can I do for you?"

"Maybe upgrade your phone for starters," she said, trying to sound funny and serious at the same time. "Other than that, I think I might have come across something. Have you thought about—"

"Now hold on, Agent White. I appreciate all you did for us while you were here and you're a damned fine agent from what I can tell. But I've been informed by your supervisor that you aren't on this case anymore. He also asked that I not contact you or speak with you should you contact me. I shouldn't have even called you back."

"When was this?"

"No more than an hour after you were gone. He said there would be two other agents coming in tomorrow to wrap things up."

"Yes, I've been texting with one of them. But Sheriff Tate, I know where—"

"Again, I'm sorry," Tate said, interrupting. "I hate to do it, but I'm hanging up now. I'm not about to go against the wishes of your supervisor."

"But—"

Mackenzie heard the click of the line going dead in her ear. She nearly called him right back, defiant and stubborn. But she finally thought better of it, doing what she could to remain responsible and clear-headed.

She also pushed aside any thoughts of calling McGrath. She wasn't sure if she wanted to give him a piece of her mind or if she wanted to pass on her hunch to him in the hopes that *he* would send them to Tate.

With a sudden burst of energy, Mackenzie got to her feet. She paced the room for a moment, pocketing her cell phone and picking her holstered Glock up from its usual place atop her dresser.

After a few moments, she walked out into the living room where Ellington was watching *Pawn Stars.* Without saying a word, Mackenzie picked up the remote control and cut the television off. She stood directly in front of him and looked down to him. For a moment, she thought she was going to cry. The words she had planned seemed to stick on the end of her tongue; she had to force it a bit in order to get them out.

"I need you to ask me again," she said softly.

It seemed as if it took Ellington a second or two to understand what she was talking about. When he finally understood, he leaned forward with a smile and took her hand. He clumsily moved from his sitting position on the couch to one knee on the floor.

"Mackenzie White…will you marry me?"

She wished hearing him say it again would have made her instantly become more vulnerable, more willing to risk fully giving herself away. And while there *was* a part of her heart that softened at the sincerity in his voice and in his expression, there was still something that didn't quite click together for her.

Still, she knew she loved him. There was no doubt of that. He made her feel safe and cherished, the sort of man who would risk coming to see her and assist with a case even after he had been suspended. The sort of man who had literally taken bullets for her.

"Yes," she said.

And rather than him stand up for her, she dropped down to her knees and embraced him. The embrace quickly became a kiss, a slow one that seemed to put a stamp on the moment. When it was broken, she looked him in the eyes, uncertain as to whether or not the next moment would require a serious tone or a comical one.

"There *is* one condition, though," she said.

"Of course there is," he replied with a smirk. "Name it."

"In about five minutes, I'm leaving to go back to Kingsville. I need you to not try to talk me out of it and not tell McGrath…though I'm sure he'll find out pretty soon one way or the other."

He thought about this for a moment, clearly not liking the way she had cornered him on the issue, but nodded. "Why are you going back?"

"I think I know where he's going next. I tried to call Tate to tell him but he won't talk to me due to McGrath's orders."

"Smart man," Ellington said with a hint of spite. "Is it dangerous? I only ask because this guy did get the drop on you once before, you know?"

She nodded. If she was being honest, getting revenge for attacking her was a small part of why she was so insistent on sticking with the case. "I know. And I can't promise anything. But if you're crazy enough to ask for my hand in marriage, you have to be crazy enough to trust me on this."

"I trust you," he said. "I'd just hate to lose you so soon after I managed to nail you down for the rest of your life."

She kissed him again, a quick playful peck this time. "Don't worry," she said. "I'm not going anywhere."

With that, she headed back into the bedroom to finish getting ready. As she did, images of Jimmy Gibbons's sketches floated through her mind—the shaded pools of blood, the mangled bodies and battered skin—and it made her wonder if maybe she wasn't as safe as she assumed at all.

CHAPTER THIRTY ONE

Dr. Jan Haggerty had first met with Jimmy Gibbons three years ago. He had come to her at the age of twenty-six, complaining of headaches, night terrors, and a state of depression that was nearly crippling. He had told her during that first meeting about his childhood—how his parents had died when their car had gone off of a bridge; how his mother had essentially ended her own life to save his.

His grandparents had raised him until the age of twelve and when his grandmother had died of breast cancer, his grandfather had been unable to raise him by himself. Jimmy had ended up in foster care, being bumped around to a few homes before heading at the age of eighteen to work in one of the last surviving grain fields on the edge of town.

She'd seen him as a well-intentioned kid, maybe dealing with a bit of a dark side. He'd expressed that side of himself in a few drawings she had seen and in a few conversations that had taken a morbid turn. He'd talked about a fear he had of turning into some monster, a monster who dwelled far too much on the death of his parents not because of his young loss, but because of his fascination with how they had died.

She'd seen no real trouble there. She'd walked him through those moments and he had seemed to always come back around.

But now she saw it. Now she saw the monster he had mentioned a few times and it made her wonder if she had done him a huge disservice by not tackling his dark side a little more aggressively.

And it's him...the person who has been killing those people from the bridge and the water tower, she thought. *How did I not see it?*

She knew where they were headed the moment he had turned onto Baxter Road. It was dark now, making it impossible to see the grain silos. But she knew they were there and she knew that at least one of them was just as high as the water tower that Jimmy had pitched Maureen Hanks from.

He'd admitted to it during the five hours he had held her captive in her home. On two occasions someone had knocked on

143

her door—both scheduled clients—and he had threatened her with the gun both times. On the second occasion, he had forced her into the chair behind her desk and placed the gun to the back of her head. She thought he was going to do it then, just pull the trigger and kill her. After all, he had spent the bulk of the afternoon talking about grotesque things. He'd explained his fascination not only with death, but with gore.

We possess these beautifully created bodies that are amazingly knit together inside, he had told her. *But when these bodies hit something hard, it all comes undone. It breaks. It unspools.*

He'd waited until it got dark to really dive deep, though. He'd made his way around the house, making her lead the way while holding the gun to her back. She expected him to be violent or even rape her. But the worst she got was a groping incident that didn't really even seem intentional.

No, he was more interested in what was to come. Even before he led her out of the house at 10 o'clock at night, she knew what he had planned for her. Her only hope was that the police had figured out what he was up to and could step in to save the day.

Yet as they sped further down Baxter Road with Jimmy behind the wheel of her car, she started to get the feeling that there would be no help. The starless night and the scattering of dark clouds in the sky seemed to echo it.

"What are you hoping to accomplish?" she asked him. "It won't make you better. It won't change the fact that your parents are dead. Jimmy, you see that, don't you?"

"I don't care about my dead parents," he said. "And you're wrong. This *does* help. I'm sleeping better. I'm not as depressed. I'm sorry, Doc…but I just like it. Others get off on drugs or sex. This is my thing. I enjoy it. Is that normal?"

"No, it's not."

She tried to keep herself from crying, but the tears came anyway. When he shrugged innocently at her comment, she knew she was in trouble. He seemed to have no conscience about this sort of thing. If it was bringing him genuine relief in some skewed and morbid way, he would fail to see the evil in it.

And in that regard, maybe he *had* become a monster.

CHAPTER THIRTY TWO

Mackenzie arrived in Kingsville at 10:08. She felt more alone than she had any of the other times she had driven into town. Maybe it was the pitch-black sky, the moon only a fingernail sliver in the sky, roaming clouds blocking out the stars. Or maybe it was because she was taking a huge roll of the dice on this. Even if her hunch was correct and she apprehended the killer, McGrath would still rain down hellfire on her. And if she was wrong—well, she and Ellington might enjoy the first few months of their engagement together with mutual suspensions.

She could not recall where Tate had said the grain silos were located, if he had ever mentioned it at all. She had to use the process of elimination, a risky choice given that the majority of Kingsville consisted of forests and back roads. Still, she did her best. She knew that the western edge of town was where the Case cornfields took over most of the land. She also knew that the grain fields were nowhere near the center of town.

She used the map on her GPS to determine that the fields were either on the eastern side of town or to the south. According to the map, everything else was covered in forest with no open expanses of land visible.

She sped down the back roads, assuming the grain fields would be to the south, where the town of Kingsville came to an abrupt end leaving nothing more than more open space and forest until the next neighboring small town took over. That's where the map seemed to show the most open land, perfect for running fields of grain.

She took the turns along the back roads at dangerous speeds, the tires screeching beneath her. She thought about calling Tate again to tell him he may as well listen to her now because she was already in town. She decided not to, not wanting to seem overly defiant of her supervisor's orders until she *knew* she was right.

Five minutes later, the canopy of forest to her left dropped away and revealed a field of grain. It was in poor shape and badly maintained, but that didn't matter. Up ahead, she saw a turn-off road that seemed to lead directly along the edge of the field. She turned onto this road—Baxter Road—and decreased her speed. As she crept along, two objects seemed to spring up out of the darkness

145

further out into the fields—almost in the same way they had appeared in Jimmy's drawings.

Two grain silos.

Simply from their shapes in the darkness, she could tell that they were old—relics, really. She knew that the newer silos were usually wide and shorter than these, often made of some kind of shiny metal. But these were from another time, probably used as early as the fifties or so. They were tall and relatively thin, ending in a dulled dome shape. If they were like the other older silos she had once seen while in Nebraska, they'd be made out of a strange mix of aluminum and concrete. While it was impossible to estimate their height, she guessed they were just as tall as the water tower. Maybe even a few feet taller.

She continued to creep along, looking for an access road. It did not take long before she saw it, a strip of dirt track that seemed to appear out of nowhere. She turned off onto this road a bit too fast, causing the undercarriage of the car to scrape the dirt. She slowed a bit and started down the road. Going purely on instinct, she killed her headlights and proceeded forward. It took he eyes a while to adjust to the absolute darkness ahead of her, but she managed to still creep along.

About five hundred yards down the road, she came to a parked car. There were two old posts on either side of the dirt track and a cable hanging between them. An ancient sign that barely read *No Trespassing* hung from the cable, riddled with bullet holes.

She pulled her car behind the parked car, wishing she could call in the tags to see who it belonged to. But honestly, the fact that there was a vehicle parked there at all was enough reason for Mackenzie to get out of her car and instantly withdraw her Glock.

The night was so quiet all around her that she could easily hear the cooling ticks of her car's engine. She made her way over the cable in the middle of the dirt track and started walking forward, into a darkness that seemed all too eager to have her.

***

Jimmy struck Dr. Haggerty for the first time when they reached the second silo. He had walked directly by the first one, making a line for the second one. He ordered her to stop walking and then, unprovoked and seemingly out of nowhere, he drew back the hand holding the gun and struck her on the back of the head.

The world swam for a moment as she went to the ground. The pain wasn't as bad as the dizziness and the sudden surge in her

146

stomach. As she tried to get to her knees, she was vaguely aware of Jimmy walking back toward the thickness of the grain. He bent down to retrieve something and she watched as he pulled a hidden ladder out of the grain. It was the sturdy sort that unhinged in the center, extending to add to the length of the ladder. As he worked on extending it, he looked back over at her to make sure she was still knocked down.

And she was. Even amidst the stark blackness of the night, she could still see the little black stars in her vision. The back of her head ached terribly, too.

Before she knew it, she felt Jimmy's hand on her arm. He gripped her tight and hauled her up to her feet. He gave a shove that nearly caused her to fall again. Wincing against the pain in the back of her head, she looked ahead and saw that in her pain and dizziness, she had missed him placing the ladder against the side of the silo. There were old iron handholds creating a ladder along the center of it but a few of them looked to have been knocked loose over time.

"Up," Jimmy said, nestling the gun into the small of her back.

For a moment, she thought of refusing. The worst he could do was shoot her and she figured she was going to die one way or another. But that was a defeatist way to think. She figured there was always the small chance that the police could show up or that Jimmy might even have a change of heart when they neared the top.

So with one last flickering beat of hope in her heart, Dr. Haggerty walked toward the ladder. With a final nudge from the gun at her back, she placed her foot on the first rung and started up.

***

Mackenzie came to the end of the thin dirt track in the grain field. Right away, she could see the slightly trampled grain in front of her, indicating that someone had passed through recently. She did not follow this disrupted path, though; she walked directly beside it, trying to dig out as many clues from the path as she could. It looked mostly like a single file path but in a few areas, she saw where it veered out a little. She took her flashlight out and hunkered down, hiding herself in the overgrown grain.

She saw the passage of two people—one ahead and one behind. And just as she made this out, she heard something in the distance up ahead. A creaking noise, like metal on metal but muted.

And then she heard a moan.

She looked toward the grain silos, now about one hundred yards ahead of her. She hurried along, still trying to remain as discreet as possible. If she could reach the silos without being seen, she'd be in good shape. She ran in a half crouch that mostly hid her body but her passage through the grain would be obvious to anyone who was bothering to look.

She heard the noise again, a screeching kind of metal-on-metal complaint. She peered ahead in the darkness and could see nothing out of the ordinary. Now that she was closer to the silos, though, she got a better idea of their shape and size. They were both the same height and looked to be slightly taller than the water tower. The darkness and distance made it hard, but she'd be surprised if they were any less than one hundred feet tall.

As she drew in closer and started to see the sides of the silos, she saw a thin structure that seemed to come off of the side of one of the silos. It went downward at an angle and appeared to have a series of struts in its center.

A ladder, Mackenzie thought. She remembered Tate saying that it was next to impossible to reach the top of the silos so she assumed a ladder would be a solution. Of course, the silos were too tall for the ladder to reach the top.

Never one to settle for speculation, Mackenzie raced a bit faster, closing in quickly. After another thirty seconds or so, the grain came to a stop. It was replaced by an overgrown area of grass, mostly populated with weeds. She had her flashlight with her but did not see the point in making herself known just yet. She ignored the first silo he came to and went directly to the second one, where the ladder was perched.

She gazed up and saw two people on the side of the silo. It was impossible to see clearly what was happening in the darkness, but it looked like the ladder had led them to the iron rungs along the side of the silo. Mackenzie saw these same rungs directly in front of her but also saw that many of these were fractured or hanging loosely from one end.

He's been out here to check it out before tonight, she thought.

Quickly, she took her phone out. She pulled up Tate's number and sent him a text. She figured he'd be more likely to habitually read an incoming text than force himself to speak with her on the phone.

Second silo. Two people going up right now. Send help.

And with the text sent, Mackenzie readied herself and started up the ladder.

CHAPTER THIRTY THREE

Mackenzie climbed the ladder as quietly as she could but the sides still made that groaning metallic sound she had heard minutes ago while she had passed through the grain field. The first time the ladder made the complaint, it was soft and barely there at all. But the second time she made it, when she was just shy of having reached the halfway point, it was louder and quite grating.

A nervous voice called out from somewhere overhead. "Who the fuck is down there?"

Mackenzie decided to stay quiet. Without any true understanding of Jimmy Gibbons, she didn't know what the thought of an FBI agent tailing him might do to him. She did stop for a moment, though, looking up to see exactly where Gibbons and his apparent next victim were located. They were very close to the top, the iron rungs coming to a stop beneath what appeared to be a very thin lip that circled the edge of the silo before the dome capped off the top.

She was pretty sure Gibbons was bringing up the rear, forcing his victim to go ahead first. He was climbing awkwardly because he seemed to be holding something in his hand. A gun, maybe. But if that was the case, she couldn't help but assume that it was just for show—that it wasn't loaded. Otherwise, he would likely have started shooting at her the moment he saw her coming.

Unless he's now dreaming of throwing two *people off,* she thought.

She knew that one well-placed shot would take him out. But she also knew that shooting from a ladder high up in the sky on a starless night where vision was murky at best would be very dangerous. She could hit the hostage. Or she might be able to hit Gibbons and on his way down, he could easily collide into her and send them both crashing to their deaths.

So until she could see a clear and present danger to the soon-to-be victim, she would take no such shot. Bringing a killer in alive and relatively unharmed was always preferable over hauling his corpse away from the scene in a body bag. Even thinking this, though, Mackenzie knew that she was going to have to move quickly. She could not rely on her assumption that Gibbons would

149

want to relish the moment before throwing his victim off. For all she knew, he'd do it the moment he reached that little walkway overhead.

She came to the end of the ladder and found that she had been right; the ladder ended just beneath where a series of sturdier iron rungs clung to the side of the silo. When her hand fell on the first one, her heart lurched. These rails were much thinner than the ones on the ladder. As she pulled herself up by them, she felt gravity trying to claim her and, for the first time, became aware of the opens space behind her.

She fought against it and continued to climb the ladder. She looked up again and saw that Gibbons and the person in front of him were nearing the lip at the top of the silo. She was going to have to speed up and hope that she could use the brief interruption when Gibbons and his victim reached the top.

But her hands seemed to be drenched in sweat and as she pushed herself faster, the rungs started to feel thinner, the open space behind her feeling as if it were physically pulling at her.

Overhead, she heard a woman's slight cry of despair, followed by what sounded like a metallic clinking. Mackenzie looked up while still scaling the side of the silo. From what she could tell, the person in front of Gibbons—a female from the sound of it—had reached the thin walkway at the top.

Mackenzie took a second to reach into the interior pocket of her coat. She pulled out the little flashlight that she had stored there before leaving DC and clicked it on. She pointed it upward to get a better view. All she could see was the bottoms of a pair of shoes roughly twenty feet overhead. As she watched, Gibbons was also coming to a stop on the rungs, reaching up and out for the thin walkway.

Mackenzie sped up, climbing with reckless abandon now. She knew that if she did not reach Gibbons by the time he got onto the walkway, she could be in trouble. All he had to do was block her entrance onto the walkway. Of course, she could shoot him—and would if she had to—but even then, firing a gun while clinging desperately to an iron rung while about eighty feet in the air did not appeal to her.

She placed the flashlight into her mouth, clamping down on it and using both hands to scale up. She neared the top and saw Gibbons throw one leg over onto the walkway. As he began to lift his other leg, Mackenzie stretched herself out, skipping the next rung in line, and made a swipe for his leg.

150

She managed to slap him along the calf but not quite hard enough. He stumbled a bit between the final rung and the walkway and cried out in surprise.

What he did next caught Mackenzie off guard. Rather than scramble up onto the walkway in fear, he held to the edge and stomped down. His left foot caught the side of her head. Reflexively, her left hand released the rung and her knees buckled at the impact. The flashlight fell from her mouth and went pinwheeling down toward the ground in a frenzy of light.

She screamed as her legs went slipping off of the rung they had been on. Her left hand dangled uselessly out into open air as her sweat-slicked right hand clung on for dear life.

Gibbons repositioned himself at the base of the walkway and drew his leg back once more. If he managed to slam it down on her right hand, she was dead.

Mackenzie swung her left hand across her chest and clumsily unholstered the Glock. She freed it and drew it, doing her best to forget the fact that she was right-handed. She didn't have time to aim but fired anyway.

The shot was loud, the recoil slight but feeling like an earthquake in her left arm as her right hand held the entire weight and life of her body.

She heard the round strike the underside of the walkway just as Gibbons yelled out in surprise and scrambled up to the top. Mackenzie swung her legs back onto the rungs and gripped the final one with her left hand, pulling herself up as well. Even before she had a good hold on the edge, she could see that it was no more than two feet wide, just wide enough for someone to walk across it.

She saw Gibbons rushing toward her, drawing his foot back to kick her. He was screaming in frustration, apparently so mad with his bloodlust that he didn't even consider the consequences. Mackenzie, still unable to switch to her firing hand, pulled off another shot. She aimed high, hoping to take out his knee, but the shot went low. It tore through his sneaker and came out the top of his foot.

He howled in pain and stumbled backward against the edge of the silo. Behind him, the woman that he had forced up the silo was slowly backing away, making a shaky retreat around to the other end of the silo.

As Gibbons bounced around on his good foot trying to reclaim his balance, Mackenzie hauled herself up onto the walkway. She was finally able to get the Glock into her right hand and when she did, she got to her feet slowly. When she took two steps away from the small opening that led back to the rungs and the nearly one-hundred-foot drop below, she finally breathed a slight sight of relief.

A *very* slight one.

It also helped that she heard sirens in the distance. Apparently, her text to Tate had worked.

Meanwhile, Gibbons took one shaky step forward, hobbling toward her. Mackenzie took another step forward to meet him, the Glock aimed straight out.

"Who are you?" he asked. He was crying, whether from the sheer absurdity of the situation itself or from the pain (or both) she wasn't certain.

"I'm Agent Mackenzie White with the FBI. Who's up here with you?"

"An old friend," he said. "A doctor. But even she couldn't help. She couldn't make the monster go away."

"Whoever is back there," Mackenzie called out to the other side of the silo, "stay where you are. You're safer back there."

"Okay," replied a vaguely familiar voice.

Gibbons looked from Mackenzie to the edge of the walkway. Mackenzie followed his gaze and saw headlights quickly approaching, highlighted by the swirling blues and reds of Kingsville PD patrol cars.

A thin safety rail stood about three feet from the platform and, honestly, didn't provide much in the way of safety at all. Seeing it at this height was almost laughable.

"You ready to shoot me?" Gibbons asked.

"If I have to."

"Good," he said. "Because someone is going off this silo."

With that, he came surging forward. He gave no warning at all. He simply ran forward, arms outstretched as if he intended to wrap her up in a bear hug. Mackenzie fired twice and sidestepped to the left, nearly colliding with the side of the silo.

The shots both took Gibbons high in the right shoulder—not fatal but painful as hell from such a close range. Shocked and dazed, he went leaning hard to the right as his legs buckled. He slapped out at her and seized the collar of her jacket. He gave a wide grin and in his eyes, there in the darkness at such a height, she thought she could see some form of the monster he had been talking about.

And then he forced himself over the safety railing.

When his free-falling weight hit the open air, his hand still held her jacket. He had it in a death grip, pulling her forward. Her hip

152

struck the safety rail and although she managed to grab it with her left hand, she still went sailing over it in an identical fashion to the near-fall she had taken at the water tower.

There was a moment of pause as her neck snapped hard to the right. Gibbons still had his hand on her jacket and she could hear the fabric tearing, but she could also feel his weight dangling from her, all transferred to her left arm. Again, her left hand was the only thing saving her from falling.

The threads popped and tore in her jacket collar but she didn't know how much longer she could hold both of their bodies' weight. She had only one option and the thought of it made her feel almost heartless.

She steeled her nerves for a fraction of a second, steadied her right arm in midair, and fired.

The shot took Jimmy Gibbons directly between the eyes. Everything in him went blank and slack, including the muscle reflexes in his hands. He released her jacket and went falling backward into all of that open space.

As he fell, the first of the patrol cars came tearing through the grain, bouncing along the rough ground. But Mackenzie was barely aware of that. She could not tear her eyes away from Gibbons as he fell. When he hit the ground about one hundred feet below, she could still feel his eyes on her.

Sobbing, she tossed her Glock up onto the walkway. She grabbed the safety rail with her right hand and the relief to her left arm was immense. As she pulled herself up, she felt a dull sensation in her left arm; she wondered if she had pulled a muscle in her desperate attempt not to fall.

But then she felt a set of hands on her right wrist. She looked up and saw Jan Haggerty there. She looked all out of sorts but managed to find enough of her wits to help Mackenzie back up onto the walkway. When her feet were resting back on that thin little lip around the silo, she sat down. She leaned against the silo wall, unable to get the haunted look she had seen in Gibbons's eyes out of her mind.

"You okay?" Mackenzie asked Haggerty.

"Yeah. For the most part. You?"

Mackenzie nodded and gave a shaky chuckle that nearly came out in a very brief bout of weeping. "Yeah," she said. "I'm just trying not to think of getting back down."

***

153

Within another half an hour, Mackenzie and Dr. Haggerty were back on solid ground. Dr. Haggerty handled herself well, not letting her trauma overrule her. She was able to tell Mackenzie and Sheriff Tate about her day without exaggerating or melting down. She told them how she had met with Jimmy Gibbons a few times in the past, mainly to talk about overcoming nightmares about his parents. She then told them about how he had essentially held her hostage for the afternoon until he had forced her to drive out to the silos.

The gun that Gibbons had been carrying *had* been empty. Apparently he had no qualms about pitching people from great heights but wasn't much in the way of shooting people.

After Tate had a look at the body lying in front of the silo, he looked to the ground like a scolded child and walked back over to Mackenzie.

"I should have taken your call," he said. "That's on me, and I'm incredibly sorry."

"It's okay," she said. "I understand why you did it. I still need to find a way to explain this without having my supervisor bite my head off."

"You need anything from us?" Tate asked. Behind him, a few other officers including Andrews and Roberts were looking around the edge of the clearing. One was running a flashlight beam up and down the ladder that was still propped up against the silo.

"Not right now. I may call you for your description of this scene for my final reports. I have a feeling I'm going to have to get pretty detailed if I want to keep my job."

"Any chance a good word from a small-town sheriff would help?" Tate asked.

"It couldn't hurt," she said.

She thanked him and shook his hand as she headed back to her car. She knew she could not go back home just yet. There was protocol to be followed. She'd need to stay until the coroner arrived, until the scene was cleared. She thought about just calling the motel and booking a room but decided not to.

She had a fiancé waiting for her back at home.

Home. It was a word that seemed to have a new meaning now that she knew what her future had for her.

In the passenger seat of her car, she grabbed her phone and called Ellington. He answered right away.

"You okay?" he asked.

"I am. The case is closed. I got him."

"What? Damn...that was quick."

He was right, but the thought of not once but *twice* dangling just a few fingers away from certain death made it seem like it had lasted an eternity.

"I'm going to be late getting home. Probably tomorrow."

"That's okay. Try to make it around lunch time if you can. That will give me time to go out and get you a ring."

It was a happy thought, one that made her feel like a winsome teenager for a moment. But then she looked back out at the silos and thought about her near falls. She looked to the crumpled body of Jimmy Gibbons and sighed. In contrast, an engagement ring seemed trivial.

"I'll see you tomorrow," she said. "I love you."

"Back at you," Ellington said, and ended the call.

Mackenzie got out of the car and approached Haggerty, who was propped against a patrol car. She saw Mackenzie coming and gave her a tired smile.

"Have I properly thanked you yet? For saving my life?"

"I don't know," Mackenzie said. She then started talking right away, not giving Haggerty the chance *to* thank her. "He referred to himself as a monster," she said. "He said you couldn't make the monster go away. What did he mean?"

"Earlier today he said that killing people was the only thing that could make him better. He said he needed to become the monster in order to make the nightmares and the depression go away."

"And do you think that's possible?" Mackenzie asked. "Do you think it's possible that men can sometimes just be evil for no reason? Just because they enjoy monstrous things?"

"I don't," Haggerty said right away. "At his heart, there was nothing evil or monstrous about Jimmy Gibbons. He'd suffered trauma at the deaths of his parents and a rough few years in his childhood. He never processed it in a healthy way and for whatever reason, this is how he chose to deal with it." She paused here and asked, "How about you?"

Slowly, Mackenzie shook her head. "I don't think so. I've seen just about every type of so-called evil man you can imagine. And like you said—at the heart of it all, there's some trauma or pain or circumstance that they were never able to deal with."

"It's sad, isn't it?" Haggerty said.

"I suppose it is," Mackenzie said. Actually, she *knew* it was. She had experienced it herself. She had never properly processed the death of her father and she had coped with it by chasing down every manner of murderer she could get her hands on.

155

For some people, becoming a monster didn't involve murderous thoughts and bloodlust. Sometimes it meant closing yourself off to everything except the ways you had to try to fix the past.

But now with her past behind her, Mackenzie had only the future to face.

And in the grain field of a starless night in a backwoods Virginia town, oddly enough, the future had never looked brighter.

CHAPTER THIRTY FOUR

Setting a date for the wedding was easy. Neither of them wanted a big wedding, nor did they have family that would care to attend. However, they also did not want to just go to the courthouse and get a license. In the end, they settled on a simple ceremony in a public garden near the National Arboretum. And while the ceremony was still two months away, there was plenty to be encouraged about in the meantime.

First, less than two weeks after Mackenzie had put Kingsville behind her, all charges were dropped against Ellington. It turned out that in the course of acquiring evidence against him, a few scandalous tidbits about his accuser had surfaced. The charges were dropped, there was absolutely no case to be had, and Ellington was reinstated pretty much on the spot.

In the months leading up to the wedding, Mackenzie did suffer from nightmares, though they were no longer about her father or anything to do with cornfields. Instead, she would find herself hanging naked from Miller Moon Bridge, starting down into a bottomless pit. The worst things about the nightmares was she always let go, allowing herself to fall into the darkness. And when she did, there was an exquisite relief to it.

She would always wake up in the nearly cliché state of being jarred awake by the sensation of falling. She saw a bureau psychiatrist about it and it was far too familiar to her, bringing back the moments in which she had tried to better understand the fear of heights while trying to track down a killer in Kingsville. It had helped for the most part but Mackenzie felt that she'd have to live with at least some degree of fear when it came to heights for the rest of her life.

At work, McGrath had only torn into her a bit for her actions at the end of the Kingsville case. Rather than suspend her, he had chosen a different form of punishment. He separated her and Ellington and assigned them with new partners for the foreseeable future. It almost made a logical kind of sense when he broke the new assignments down: she would be working with Yardley while Ellington would be paired with Harrison.

While it made her cringe to think about working in the field with someone other than Ellington, she saw it as yet another step in getting on with her future—in evolving her career and her life to where it needed to be to successfully put the past behind her.

Besides…even with a new partner, she and Ellington always reunited back at their apartment. There was a ring on her finger, floral arrangements to choose, and a song to select for the first dance—which was becoming quite the argument among them. She wanted something by Liz Phair, and he wanted some overplayed Rolling Stones song.

It quickly became a joke… that had they known one another's musical tastes much better, they would have never gotten engaged in the first place. And it was jokes that like those that made Mackenzie realize that it was really happening. She was going to marry this man and they'd go running into an uncertain future together.

It made her think of the relief she felt in those nightmares when she would let go of the side of Miller Moon Bridge and just drop.

Apparently, it felt good to just *let go* sometimes.

***

Three weeks before the wedding, Mackenzie was standing in the bathroom of a condo they had rented. She could hear the waves crashing on the beach outside along the coast. They had rented a place out in Sandy Point, Maryland, one of their rare weekends off of work at the same time.

She stood in front of the toilet and looked at the pregnancy test on the sink. She had no idea what she wanted the result to be. All she knew for certain was that she was terrified.

She waited, the two minutes following the test's activation dragging on and on. She could only imagine what Ellington was feeling outside as he sat on the edge of the bed, waiting.

When the result came up, she walked slowly to the test. She took a moment to sort through her own emotions before picking it up and walking out of the bathroom. Ellington stood up with the speed of a jack-in-the-box, his eyes tracking directly to the test.

She handed it to him and watched his eyes. She could not read them. Despite their time together, it always surprised her when he was able to contain his emotions so well. *Job hazard,* he always told her.

"Negative," he said.

"Yes. Negative."

He handed the test back to her, as if he had no idea what he was holding. "How do you feel about that?" he asked.

"Good," she said. "But I think I would have been good if it had come out positive, too."

"Yeah?"

She nodded. "I don't *want* one now, but...well, some day."

Ellington sat back down on the bed and pulled her to him. "I think I do, too. It's just hard to fathom it with everything we see, every day, day in and day out."

"So maybe we start with a dog," she said. "But nothing small or frou-frou."

"Now you're talking," Ellington said.

He pulled her onto the bed and they spent the next hour there.

When they were done, Mackenzie dozed. And during her nap, she dreamed.

She was standing on the front stoop of the house from her childhood. She knew that she was a little girl in the dream. She knew this because her father was there, not dead and not in some grotesque state as he had been in previous dreams. Instead, he was standing on the porch, watching her walk down into the yard. She was carrying the little BB gun that he'd purchased for her at a yard sale. In the front yard was a series of cans that he had set up for her.

It was her very first shooting range. In the dream, she pumped the BB gun, taking great pride in each pump.

"Careful with that thing," her dad said. "Don't shoot your eye out. Or a window. Your mom would kill me. Hell...she'll kill me for buying it for you anyway."

"How do I make sure I shoot where I want to shoot?" Mackenzie asked.

"The sight," he said. He came down from the porch and stood behind her. He helped her hold the gun correctly and then pointed out the sight at the end of the barrel. "You line the cans up with this little tab here at the end of the barrel. And when it's all lined up, you shoot."

She did as instructed and when she pulled the trigger, there was about half a second that passed and then an empty can of peas went rolling over.

"Good shot!" he told her, wrapping an arm around her.

She blushed, soaking in the words of praise from her dad. She lined up her next shot and blasted another can. And then another and another.

"Looks like I won't have to worry about you taking care of yourself when you get older," he said. "It looks like you can hold your own!"

Mackenzie White woke up with that comment from her father spiraling through her head. She looked at Ellington and was glad that he, too, had dozed off. She wasn't so much embarrassed that she had fallen asleep in the middle of the day as she was at the innocence of the dream. She was crying and could not quite explain why.

She got out of bed and walked to the balcony window, standing by the sliding doors. She looked out to the beach, watching people walk up and down. A girl was flying a kite. A family was playing a game of corn hole.

There were lives taking place out there, people she did not know with dreams she could not even begin to imagine.

But she looked past them all and to the limitless expanse of the ocean. The horizon was a blur from where she stood and something about that comforted her. Even something as absolute and as solid as the horizon could be blurred. And no matter how close you got to it, it always moved with you, always the same distance away.

There *were* things that remained constant despite the circumstances.

And with a ring on her finger, a man holding her heart, and the demons of her past finally buried and behind her, she was ready for some consistency.

BEFORE HE LONGS
(A Mackenzie White Mystery—Book 10)

From Blake Pierce, #1 bestselling author of ONCE GONE (a #1 bestseller with over 1,200 five star reviews), comes BEFORE HE LONGS, book #10 in the heart-pounding Mackenzie White mystery series.

BEFORE HE LONGS is book #10 in the #1 bestselling Mackenzie White mystery series, which begins with BEFORE HE KILLS (Book #1), a #1 bestseller with over 500 reviews!

FBI Special Agent Mackenzie White is summoned when another body is found dead in a self storage unit. There at first appears to be no connection between the cases; yet as Mackenzie digs deeper, she realizes it is the work of a serial killer—and that he will soon strike again.

Mackenzie will be forced to enter the mind of a madman as she tries to understand a psyche obsessed with clutter, storage, and claustrophobic places. It is a dark place from which she fears she may not return—and yet one which she must probe if she has any chance of winning the game of cat and mouse that can save new victims.

Even then, it may be too late.

A dark psychological thriller with heart-pounding suspense, BEFORE HE LONGS is book #10 in a riveting new series—with a beloved new character—that will leave you turning pages late into the night.

Blake Pierce

Blake Pierce is author of the bestselling RILEY PAGE mystery series, which includes twelve books (and counting). Blake Pierce is also the author of the MACKENZIE WHITE mystery series, comprising eight books (and counting); of the AVERY BLACK mystery series, comprising six books; and of the new KERI LOCKE mystery series, comprising five books.

An avid reader and lifelong fan of the mystery and thriller genres, Blake loves to hear from you, so please feel free to visit www.blakepierceauthor.com to learn more and stay in touch.

BOOKS BY BLAKE PIERCE

THE MAKING OF RILEY PAIGE SERIES
WATCHING (Book #1)

RILEY PAIGE MYSTERY SERIES
ONCE GONE (Book #1)
ONCE TAKEN (Book #2)
ONCE CRAVED (Book #3)
ONCE LURED (Book #4)
ONCE HUNTED (Book #5)
ONCE PINED (Book #6)
ONCE FORSAKEN (Book #7)
ONCE COLD (Book #8)
ONCE STALKED (Book #9)
ONCE LOST (Book #10)
ONCE BURIED (Book #11)
ONCE BOUND (Book #12)
ONCE TRAPPED (Book #13)

MACKENZIE WHITE MYSTERY SERIES
BEFORE HE KILLS (Book #1)
BEFORE HE SEES (Book #2)
BEFORE HE COVETS (Book #3)
BEFORE HE TAKES (Book #4)
BEFORE HE NEEDS (Book #5)
BEFORE HE FEELS (Book #6)
BEFORE HE SINS (Book #7)
BEFORE HE HUNTS (Book #8)
BEFORE HE PREYS (Book #9)
BEFORE HE LONGS (Book #10)

AVERY BLACK MYSTERY SERIES
CAUSE TO KILL (Book #1)
CAUSE TO RUN (Book #2)
CAUSE TO HIDE (Book #3)
CAUSE TO FEAR (Book #4)
CAUSE TO SAVE (Book #5)
CAUSE TO DREAD (Book #6)